FIGHT THE SHOCK

WILLIAM ODAY

William Oday, November 2019
Copyright © 2019 William Oday
All rights reserved worldwide

All rights reserved. With the exception of excerpts for reviews, no part of this book may be reproduced or transmitted in any form or by any means, electronic or mechanical, including photocopying, recording, or by any information storage and retrieval system.

This is a work of fiction. Names, characters, places, dialogues, and incidents either are the product of the author's imagination or are used fictitiously. Any resemblance to actual events, locations, or persons, living or dead, is purely coincidental.

ISBN-13: 978-1942472278

1

The plane shuddered through yet another pocket of turbulent air. Cade Bowman liked flying about as much as he liked dying, which was to say that he considered them to be close enough to be one and the same.

The fact that he'd flown and survived so many times over the years did nothing to change that opinion.

He gripped the armrests so hard the veins in his forearms bulged beneath the skin. He swallowed to keep from losing fifteen dollars worth of a cheese and crackers plate. He didn't normally spring for airplane food because it was always overpriced and usually tasted terrible. But it had sounded better than another energy bar from his Get Home Bag. So he'd splurged and was now determined to keep those expensive calories down.

Two months working construction in Seattle had paid well and put some padding into a depleted bank account. The time away from his wife and kids had been tough, but at least they could catch up on bills and have some room to breathe. A connecting flight in San Francisco and then he'd be on the way home to Durango, Colorado.

He couldn't wait.

An elderly lady sitting next to him patted his hand. Her skeletal fingers cold and light as a feather touch. "It's going to be okay, dear. I take this flight every summer to visit my grandson in San Francisco, and I always get there. Now, two summers ago was a real headache, let me tell you. Or was it three? Anyway, there was a problem with the plane and they made us wait on the tarmac for hours. They wouldn't even let people get up to go to the bathroom. I'm sorry, but when you get to be my age you simply can't hold it forever. But did they care? No. Can you believe that?"

Cade forced a smile and then grimaced when another pocket of rough air shook the plane.

The intercom crackled. "Ladies and gentlemen, this is your captain speaking. We're beginning our descent to San Francisco International Airport. As you've noticed, we're moving through some turbulence, so hang tight and we'll be below it in a few minutes. Once again, on behalf of American Airlines and the crew, it's a pleasure to have you with us and we hope to see you again soon. Flight crew, please prepare for arrival."

Cade looked out the window and saw the city in the distance. Twinkling lights through a thick blanket of fog. Unfortunately, he also saw the black void of the bay as well. The pinprick lights of boats here and there punctuated the vast stretches of darkness between. He didn't enjoy flying in the first place and flying over large bodies of water at night was even worse. His phone lit up. A text from his wife, Samantha.

Call me when you can. Love you.

He texted back. He wasn't supposed to have his phone on, but he'd forgotten to set it to airplane mode. And they were obviously low enough for it to pick up a signal.

Will do. Love you too.

He decided to send another.

And don't stress. We'll figure it out like we always—

The screen went dark.

The cabin lights did too, plunging the interior

into darkness.

The plane dropped and Cade's stomach flopped, the queasy feeling of plunging down a roller coaster.

Voices rose in panic. Some broke into screams.

He sunk into his seat as the plane leveled out some, but it was still angled down far more than it should've been.

"What's happening?" someone yelled.

"We're gonna crash!" another voice added.

Cade clenched his torso tight and groaned through the surge of adrenaline, fighting to keep the rising fear in check.

A hand latched onto his arm and slid down.

He peeled his fingers off the armrest and clasped the old woman's hand. He wanted to reassure her, tell her it was going to be okay, but it was all he could do to keep himself under control. Instead, he held her frail hand in his and squeezed, but not too hard. A career in the trades had made his body strong and his grip like iron. Some tasks required brute strength. This one required a subtler touch.

A door slammed somewhere ahead and a frantic voice yelled above the din. "Ladies and gentlemen, please remain calm! We've lost power and will have to make an emergency landing in the bay. Life jackets are below your seats. Please do not inflate—"

Her words were drowned out by a new wave of screaming and shouting. Terror filled the cabin with a palpable, suffocating weight.

Cade reached beneath his seat but couldn't find anything that felt like a life jacket that could be removed. Years ago, he'd once taken the time to locate the vest and run through how to retrieve it and put it on. But that wasn't helping now because it wasn't there. Or maybe it was tucked somewhere that wasn't obvious in the dark.

A soft voice whispered in his ear. "Our father who art in heaven, hallowed be Thy name..."

Cade hadn't been all that religious since leaving the church as a teenager, but he joined the woman in prayer, silently speaking the parts he remembered.

They finished it together and Cade added a prayer of his own.

Please let me live. I have a wife, a daughter, and a son who need me. Please, God, let me be there for them.

A shadow hurried by in the aisle. "Put your heads down, arms around your legs and brace for impact! Put your heads down, arms around your legs and brace for impact!"

Cade snatched his bag from below the seat in front and stuffed it down at his side. He leaned over, doing his best to keep his breathing slow and steady even as his heart ran wild in his chest.

"Mommy, what's happening? I don't want to die! Mommy!" a young voice wailed over and over.

The elderly woman spoke in a strained whisper. "If the Lord takes me, tell my grandson that I love him."

"You'll tell him yourself when we get through this," Cade said through gritted teeth.

"Please, tell him for me."

What was he supposed to say?

"Okay, I will."

It wasn't important that he didn't know her grandson's name or address or anything. It was about comforting her in what could be their final moments together.

"Thank you."

Cade's body pressed down as the descent flattened out and the front of the plane lifted. He grunted through the pressure until it eased.

For a few seconds, time froze.

The plane was neither falling nor climbing.

And then the curse of the present slammed into gear as the rear of the plane hit the water. The fuselage quaked and shivered.

The seatbelt dug into his waist from the abrupt

deceleration. The front of the plane dropped and it felt like the belt was about to cut him in half. Blood filled his head. His heart thumped in his ears.

Like a bucking bull, the cabin thrashed around as the plane bounced along the surface of the bay. Overhead compartments flew open hurling bags into the aisle and onto passengers.

Cade held onto the woman's hand, probably gripping too tight but he couldn't tell. His foot hit the floor and bounced a knee back into his face. His nose erupted in white-hot pain and warm blood spilled over his lips.

The terrible shaking began to settle as the plane slowed.

Amidst the crying and yelling, a single voice cheered. Howling joyous whoops that spoke to the gift of life snatched from the jaws of death.

Cade sat up and glanced at the old woman. The pale light of the full moon coming through the window cast a dim blue glow onto her face.

She pointed past him.

He turned to look out the window just as a massive barge filled with shipping containers sheared the wing off and smashed through the tail of the plane.

2

The impact spun the plane around. The momentum snapped Cade's head to the side, shutting him off like a light.

He was somewhere else.

Home.

It was a bright and clear summer afternoon in the Rocky Mountains. He turned in circles, dazed and disoriented.

He was in a meadow swathed in lush green. A gentle breeze rippled through the grass, drawing patterns that made it feel alive and expressive. Almost like it was trying to tell him something. Majestic peaks painted an angular pattern along the horizon. The rise and fall of the lines like the scrawl of a heartbeat writ large. Sweet mountain air filled his chest. Air that could be found nowhere else in the world as far as he was concerned.

And there on a patchwork quilt made by his grandmother was all that mattered in the world.

His family. Samantha, Lily, and Ethan. Dennis, their rescued Boxer mutt, bounded out of the grass like a deer and flopped down to get his belly rubbed. It was a ridiculous name for a dog, but there was a story behind it.

The suffused rays of the sun cast a glowing halo through his wife's light brown hair. She was an angel. His angel. She saw him and a beautiful smile spread across her face. The warmth in it a reflection of the sun. Lily and Ethan laughed and waved him over to see something they'd found in the meadow.

He started toward them, but found his limbs numb and pushing through viscous air. As much as he tried, he got no closer.

The weather shifted. Clouds closed in, blocking out the sun. Darkness gathered. The air turned cold and a gust sent shivers up his spine.

They were scared now. Frantically waving and shouting, trying to tell him something but he couldn't hear what above the roar of the wind. Dennis barked wildly like he did every time a package was delivered to their front door.

Cade snapped awake with a sharp intake of air. One sensation dominated the others.

Cold.

An aching, bone-biting chill like his feet were locked inside a block of ice. A high-pitched whine like a tuning fork smacked by a hammer vibrated inside his head. A numbing distance that threatened to draw him down. Promised to make it all go away if only he would surrender.

No!

He tried to sit up, but something heavy on his back had him pinned down against his knees. He blinked and tried to focus. Took a few breaths to steady himself.

The plane.

The crash.

The barge.

It all snapped into focus with terrifying clarity.

Screams of terror choked the air. Gurgling water rushed into the cabin as the rear of the fuselage dipped below the surface of the bay.

He gathered himself and pushed against whatever was holding him down.

A lifeless body rolled off. An arm dragged across his head as the corpse splashed into the water at his feet.

He jerked away and winced as the seatbelt pinched into his waist. His hands reached for the buckle and ran into the something.

His bag.

He still had it!

He dug under it, found the buckle and got free.

The water was coming in fast now. A rushing current under the seats. He glanced out the window at the moonlight reflecting off the water. A wave splashed against the glass and then it went dark as it sank below the surface.

He remembered the elderly woman and turned to her. Fumbling in the dark, he found her slumped over. Not moving. He pulled her upright and tried to release the seatbelt.

The plane lurched and began to roll over.

He lost hold of her and she slumped forward. She was gone.

And he would be too if he didn't get out of there.

He slung the bag over his shoulder so both hands could be free.

The plane continued rolling as he climbed over the seat and started toward the back. It settled and now the opposite row of windows was the floor.

He continued on toward the half-circle at the back of the plane that was still above water.

Moonlight filtered through the row of windows above, casting everything in muted shades of blue and black.

A hand grabbed his wrist and he saw a teenage girl trapped beneath a body in a dark suit. She was around the same age as his daughter. "Help me! Please!"

He braced his boots on two armrests and heaved at the corpse. He was able to pull it up enough for her to squeeze out. "Go!" he yelled as he guided her toward a shrinking window of salvation.

A few others were climbing toward the back. Far more were trapped or dazed or already dead. A flailing limb struck out as he scrambled over twisted seats, piles of luggage and bodies.

He wanted to stop and help.

But he couldn't.

The water was rushing in faster now. Soon, it would fill the interior and the plane and everyone inside would get sucked down into the dark depths.

He kept going.

Closer now to escape.

Twenty feet from where the fuselage had been torn in two.

He was swimming as much as climbing through the rising water and the shrinking pocket of air.

A face in the water shouted to him. Only the mouth, nose and eyes above the surface.

"I'm stuck! The belt won't open! The water—" He gagged and spluttered as water poured into his mouth.

Cade reached below the surface and found the clasp. The metal was bent and the lever jammed. He clutched it like a clam, fingertips hurting, and wrenched it open. He shoved the kid forward as a wave of water swept in and sealed their escape. "Take a deep breath!" he shouted.

He did so himself and then dove under as it hit.

Only one thought remained.

Get out. Now.

He swam and climbed and made it to the ragged opening. His chest ached as the urge to breathe grew. He kicked away from the sinking hulk and made for the surface.

Chest burning for air, he broke through with a coughing, spluttering gasp. Several more before his heaving chest calmed.

Out in the middle of the bay.

Surrounded by dark water, floating debris and carnage from the crash.

And then something bumped into him.

3

Cade flinched away as the image of a shark flashed through his mind.

He spun around and found a couple of floating seat cushions. He stacked them up and hooked his arms through the straps on the back. He slowed his breathing, rising and falling with the passing swells.

He kicked around in a circle to get his bearings.

Splashing and yelling from other survivors. Not close enough to see, but not many by the sounds of it.

A body face-down in the water drifted by.

Cade gritted his chattering teeth and tried not to think about what could be swimming under the surface. What could track the blood trail to an easy meal.

There were many reasons he lived in Durango, Colorado. Distance from oceans hadn't been on the list, but it was now.

He spotted the towering silhouettes of the skyscrapers of downtown San Francisco ahead and the span of the Bay Bridge to the left. The city was dark but for a raging fire in the distance. The glowing orange flames reached high into the night sky. The hills of the city were a sea of shadows of varying depths. The light of the moon reflecting here and there, offering some illumination.

But no street lights.

No office lights checkering the sides of buildings.

No headlights snaking through the streets.

No brake lights coupled in the opposite directions.

It was dark like no city had been in well over a hundred years.

Cade heard splashing nearby and another jolt of adrenaline spiked his heart rate as he imagined sharks arriving to tear into him.

But it was another survivor.

The twenty-something kid he'd gotten free of the seatbelt. Dark hair with curls plastered to his face. Thrashing around like he'd never been in water deeper than a bathtub.

Cade swam over and the kid tried to climb him like a tree. He got dragged under before he managed to break free and get back to the surface.

The kid reached for him again.

"Stop!" Cade bellowed in his face. He shoved one of the seat cushions at him. "Get on that and take a few breaths!"

The kid complied, but Cade could see he was barely holding it together.

"What's your name?"

"We're going to get eaten by sharks, aren't we?"

That was the last thing Cade wanted to talk about. "What is your name?" he repeated, this time emphasizing each word.

The kid's head stopped bouncing around and finally settled on Cade. "Hudson."

"Hudson what?"

"Hudson McKinney."

"Okay, Hudson McKinney. We're going to survive this, but you've gotta keep your head on straight. Got it?"

"How? We're stranded out in the middle of the ocean." The panic was again taking over. "We're going to die out here!"

Cade grabbed his cushion and pulled him close. He pointed at the dark city. "See that?"

Hudson nodded.

"We're going to swim there."

"What if I can't?"

"Do your legs work?"

"Yeah."

Cade spun him around and aimed him at what looked like the nearest outcropping of land.

"Then start kicking because we either get to shore or the current's going to drag us out into the Pacific Ocean."

Hudson didn't need any more encouragement than that. He started off in a frenzy of splashing.

"Keep your feet under the water!" Cade yelled as he swam alongside. One, swimming like that wasted a lot of power. And two, sharks were attracted to thrashing movement as it typically indicated injured prey.

Hudson's kicks smoothed out and soon they were making progress toward the distant shore.

Cade settled into the rhythm of the movement. The exertion warmed his body and his chattering teeth quieted. Too soon, thoughts arose that did absolutely no good whatsoever.

They were surrounded by endless black water, and who knew what was lurking in the depths below.

A jagged-edged fear started to build in his gut, but he gritted his teeth and shut it down. The only way he was going to make it was to keep it together and keep going.

They'd been swimming for what seemed like hours when Hudson stopped and fell behind.

Cade paused and glanced over his shoulder. "What are you doing?"

"We're never going to make it! I'm exhausted. I've got nothing left."

Cade surveyed the shore and the kid had a point. It still looked so far away and the current was inexorably dragging them closer to the Golden Gate bridge and the open ocean beyond. But he knew from a lifetime of hiking in the Rocky Mountains that you could see something in the distance and it could feel like you weren't making any progress for a long time. But if you kept going, there would eventually come a point when you'd look up and realize you were almost there.

This was no different.

Or so he hoped.

"What's the most important thing in the world to you?"

By the look on Hudson's face, the question clearly caught him off guard. "My fiancé, Amelia."

"Okay. I want you to picture her face when she finds out you're dead. Think about her pain."

He was quiet as he wrestled with competing emotions.

Cade waited. But he couldn't much longer. Either this kid had to choose to fight or give up and die.

"You're an asshole," Hudson said as he started kicking again.

"Sometimes."

They continued on for another interminable stretch, but then it happened.

The dark silhouettes of the city rose into the air above them. A marina filled with boats off to the left. Ahead was some kind of naval ship straight out of World War II.

"Come on! We're almost there!" Cade yelled over his shoulder.

One last push and they made it into a protected cove. A sandy beach with gently lapping waves rolling in and out.

Cade stood on the sandy bottom and unwound his arms from the cushion. He pushed it away and staggered out of the water. He continued on above the waterline and then fell to his knees. He dropped his bag and took a second to gather his wits. Sand coated his skin like a fine grit sandpaper and already he could feel the wet clothes leeching the heat out of his body.

Hudson collapsed next to him and sobbed. Uncontrollable spasms as he let out the horror of what had just happened. "I didn't think I was going to make it." His words came out in staccato, shuddering bursts.

Cade peered into the darkness of the city that sprawled out before them. He wondered if anyone else would survive. If the girl he'd helped had gotten out.

In the distance, a crash of shattering glass was followed by the terrified shriek of a woman.

Hudson bumped into him. "What was that?"

"Don't know. Not close enough to worry about."

"What kind of power outage knocks out cars too? How is that even possible?"

Cade knew how it was possible. It was something he'd read about and hoped would never happen. His phone had cut off. The plane had shut down. The enormous fire likely another downed plane. The entire city had gone dark.

There was only one explanation that made any sense.

Arguably the worst disaster that could happen.

"We've been hit with an EMP."

His mind jumped to the next conclusion. His daughter was in Las Vegas with a friend. He knew their hotel and room number. Considering the proximity, the EMP would've taken out that city too.

Which meant she was in danger.

Terrible danger.

One way or another, he had to get to Vegas as soon as possible.

4

The elevator doors opened and Lillian Bowman stepped out onto the viewing deck of the Eiffel Tower Experience in Las Vegas. Then she turned around and went back in because she had to drag her best friend out. "You're not going to die, Piper."

"You don't know that!" Piper said as she leaned back and her black strappy heels skidded over the floor. A tight, black knit dress showed off her ample curves, which was exactly the point.

"Stop being a baby. You're going to be fine."

"It's called survival instinct and it's not my fault that you don't have it."

Lily managed to shuffle her friend out onto the viewing deck and waited for the doors to close behind them in case Piper decided to make a dash for it. With the doors closed and the elevator heading down, she let go and approached the metal mesh that enclosed the platform. She ran her fingers over the screen, thinking it was basically the same kind of hog wire that people used for fences back home in Durango.

Piper edged up behind her. "I feel like a bird."

"Because we're up so high?"

They were over four hundred feet in the air with the bright neon lights of the city below stretching out in every direction. A cool breeze a promise of the colder temperatures to come.

"No, because we're in a bird cage."

Lily looked around and it did look strikingly like a bird cage with the wire mesh coming up from the floor and wrapping overhead to the central column that housed the elevator. "It's cool, huh?"

Piper snorted. "That wasn't the thought running through my mind, no."

Lily grasped the mesh and peered south along the strip to see if she could make out their hotel. She wasn't positive, but she thought she saw a sliver of the parking garage between two buildings. Her mother's old Volvo 240 station wagon was somewhere on level five. They'd driven it here the night before.

Her mother called it reliable. She and Piper called it the Beige Barfinator. It was so ugly, other station wagons made fun of it. That was the joke, anyway. Not one they ever shared with her mother because they didn't want to lose the privilege of using it.

She gazed down at the bustle of activity on the strip far below. She liked it better from a distance. Growing up in Colorado, she'd fallen in love with the land. Hiking, fishing, hunting. There was plenty to do in and around Durango, but those were her favorites. She didn't wear Wranglers and cowboy boots—not her style—but she was nevertheless a country girl to the core.

Not that she had much of a style, as her best friend since second grade frequently noted. Piper called her style practical, and it wasn't a compliment. Brown was her favorite color, because *practical*. Brown didn't stain as easily as bright colors and it didn't have something to prove like black. Brown trail shoes, tan cargo pants and a chocolate brown moisture-wicking long sleeve shirt.

So what if her style was a practical mashup of REI and Costco?

Las Vegas shared Piper's distaste for anything practical, which was part of the reason why Lily had never had any desire to visit. If it weren't for this weekend being Piper's bachelorette party, she never would've come. And she still wouldn't have come if Melanie and Skylar hadn't bailed. She didn't blame them. Life happened. Ironically, they were both bummed not to be here while Lily was the total opposite.

Still, this particular attraction was worth a visit. Sure, it was a half-size Eiffel Tower in the heart of Las Vegas instead of Paris. But it was still amazing. She'd always dreamed of visiting the city of love with a special someone.

There were only two problems with that. Okay, probably more, but there were two big problems. One was that a vacation to Paris was insanely expensive and her family had never been exactly rolling in the dough. And money had been especially tight ever since Grams got sick.

Got sick.

That made it sound like the flu or something where she might get better.

Parkinson's wasn't like that. People didn't recover like getting over the flu. It was a long, slow excruciating decline. And they were right in the middle of it.

So, this Eiffel Tower in Sin City was the closest

she was going to get to the real one in the city of love. The other problem was that she hadn't dated anyone since breaking up with Colton nearly a year ago. She'd moved on and was ready to jump into the dating pool again if and when she found the right person.

Colton, on the other hand, somehow still harbored the delusion that they would get back together. He'd gone full stalker mode. Always asking her friends how she was doing. Driving slowly by the house. She'd told her dad about it. Big mistake. He confronted Colton one time and would've beat the crap out of him if her mother hadn't been there to stop it.

So, this Eiffel Tower was pretty awesome considering the real one wasn't an option.

Piper spun her around and wrapped her in an embrace. "Kiss me, my darling!" She leaned in for a ridiculously theatrical kiss, but Lily pulled away. Piper put her hands on her hips and struck a petulant pose. "Are you rejecting me? Is it over between us?"

She was such a drama queen. Always had been. It was funny, most of the time.

Lily noticed several of the surrounding people

watching and flashed Piper the *Do not embarrass me!* look that they both knew so well.

Piper responded with the *Gah, I was just kidding!* look that they also knew so well.

"Can we just enjoy the view for a few minutes?" Lily asked as she turned back to the screen.

"As long as it's just a few minutes. I will never forgive you if we miss a single minute of the show."

"Don't remind me." Against her better judgement, she'd agreed to go to a male dance revue. The ones where muscle head guys strip off their clothes and do ridiculous things in front of a horde of screaming women. She gagged a little thinking of it.

Lily pushed it out of her mind. She was the maid of honor and here to ensure the bride-to-be had a great time while also staying out of trouble.

She rested her forehead against the mesh and breathed in the night. The pale moon above, so small and sad compared to the glaring, glitzy lights below. Passenger jets came and went to McCarran Airport to the south. The flat desert encircled the patchwork grid of the glowing city.

Directly below, the spectacular fountains of the Bellagio built toward a climactic ending. The colored columns of water swaying to the score of classical music that they could hear all the way up there. The red lights of cars going one direction and the yellow lights of others going the opposite way. Like strings of Christmas lights. Uncurled stripes from a candy cane. Crowds of people bunched up at street corners, then spilled into the street when the traffic lights changed.

So many people.

Too many.

As good as it was to be there for her best friend, Lily was definitely looking forward to being back home in the mountains.

The Bellagio's show of water and lights was going all out now. The music booming and the fountains blasting sprays that drifted with the wind as they fell back into the enormous pool. The occasional puff of mist tickled her face.

"Admit it," Piper said. "You're happy I talked you into coming."

Lily was about to throw her a bone and say yes when something happened.

The fountains went dark and the music cut off. The glaring lights of the strip went dark. The holiday lighting of the crawling traffic snapped off. The entire city blinked off. It was like someone hit a giant light switch that controlled everything.

For a few seconds, it was totally silent. Or maybe

Lily didn't hear anything because her brain couldn't compute what was happening.

And then the sounds rushed in all at once.

Cars crashing on the street below. A few with lights still on, now spotlighted by the sea of surrounding shadows. People screaming. Worried mutterings from the other people on the observation deck.

A quiet voice whispered in her ear. "What just happened?"

Lily's brain was still trying to catch up.

And when it did, the realization that arrived sent a chill up her spine.

Her dad had said something like this could happen, but she'd never thought much about it. It was too far away and too unbelievable to matter. But looking out across the city that had seconds ago been saturated with a rainbow of light, she knew the impossible had just happened.

And worse, she remembered what he said would happen next.

She turned to Piper and grabbed her shoulder, harder than she meant to.

"We have to get out of the city."

5

Lily dug into her pocket and pulled out her phone. She tapped the screen on but couldn't get a signal. "Does your phone work?"

Piper was just staring through the mesh at the chaos unfolding below.

"Piper, does your phone work?"

She slowly turned, not all there.

"Try your phone. See if it works."

"Okay," she mumbled as she pulled it out of her purse. "Hang on. It's rebooting... Strange. It had three bars a minute ago."

Lily retrieved a headlamp from her backpack. She was about to flick it on, but then stopped. If she turned it on, the other dozen or so people would notice and maybe one of them might wonder if she had anything else useful in the bag. Maybe they would try to take it to find out.

How long before people turned on each other to get what they needed?

Like anything, it depended on the person and the situation. Good people and bad people lived everywhere. It was just that a big city had a lot more of both. And Las Vegas was a big city like no other. It was a magnet for the desperate and deluded. There was a darkness that lurked beneath the skin-deep gloss.

Lily had a bad feeling that the hidden side of Las Vegas was going to come out front and center. She pulled Piper close and whispered in her ear. "Listen to me. This is serious. I think it was an EMP, and—"

"What's an EMP?" Piper blurted out.

"Be quiet," Lily hissed in her ear. "We don't want anyone up here freaking out."

"Okay," she whispered. "But what is that?"

"It stands for electromagnetic pulse. It can happen from a solar flare or from a high altitude detonation of a nuclear bomb."

"A nuclear—"

"Shhhhh!"

"The power went out. That's all!" Piper said.

"Have you ever heard of a power outage shutting down cars? How about basically all of them?"

Piper didn't answer. Of course, she hadn't. No one had. Regular power outages didn't do that.

"You think we were attacked?" Piper whispered.

"I don't know and it doesn't matter right now. What matters is we have to get to the ground and get out of the city."

"Get down? We're over four hundred feet in the air!"

"Lower your voice!" Lily hissed.

"We have to wait for someone to come help us. They'll get the power back on and then we'll get down."

Lily shook her head. "You're not getting it. The power isn't coming back on. Not anytime soon. My dad's the expert on it, not me. But he said that power would be down for a long time. The pulse is picked up by power lines that act like giant antennas. It fries transformers and anything connected to the grid. Lights, computers, refrigerators, whatever. Anything that uses microchips is especially vulnerable, which is almost everything these days."

"That doesn't mean help won't come."

"Look down there," Lily said. Out of the hundreds of cars lining the strip, only a few still had headlights on. One of them was roaring down the sidewalk, mowing over whoever was unlucky enough to be in the way. Several cars were burning like bonfires. A doomed figure engulfed in flames stumbled away from one. A human torch with arms flailing, and then the person collapsed on the pavement and stopped moving. The screams of the dying and injured echoed in the air.

A burst of gunshots made Lily duck. She pulled Piper close again. "No one is coming for us. Every first responder in the city is going to have their hands full."

"No, they'll get a firetruck over here and use one of those extendable ladder things."

"You're not getting it," Lily hissed. "No firetrucks are going anywhere for anybody. They don't work. Just like all those cars down there."

Piper sucked in a shuddering breath. She was starting to understand. "What are we going to do?"

"We have to get down from here. It was over a hundred degrees this afternoon. It'll be the same tomorrow. We can't survive that without water."

"But you have water in that survival bag of yours. I saw you stash it on the way out of the hotel."

"Shhh!" Lily squeezed her shoulder. She didn't want to be that way, but Piper had to wrap her head around the situation and do it immediately. "Yes, I have two bottles. My canteen and a plastic bottle from our room. I doubt that would be enough for us, and it definitely wouldn't be enough for everyone up here."

"We don't have to tell anyone about it."

"Come on, Piper. Someone will see at some point. And then what do you think would happen?"

Piper looked surprised and glanced around at the huddled and terrified clusters of people. "You think they'd attack us?"

"My dad says desperation can make good people do things they wouldn't ever normally do. Besides, even if they don't, are you going to be okay with letting people pass out from dehydration while we're sipping away on our secret stash?"

"How are we going to get down then?"

This was the part Lily had been waiting for. She'd noticed it on the way up, but hadn't thought much about it until a minute ago.

"We have to get the elevator doors open and climb down the maintenance ladder."

"What?" Piper blurted out. "Are you insane?"

The shadowed faces of several of the others pivoted toward them, but then turned back to their own concerns.

Fight the Shock

"It's the only way down."

"No! One slip and it's over. You're definitely insane."

Lily dug into her pack and pulled out a hundred foot bundle of olive green cord.

"What's that?"

"It's 550 paracord. I'll use it to tie us together. It's just for backup."

Piper did not look convinced.

Which was understandable because Lily wasn't all that confident either. But it was better than nothing and with the prospect of baking up here the only alternative, it would have to do.

Someone bumped into Lily's back, nearly knocking her over. She caught herself and looked up.

Pungent fumes washed over them as a huge guy wearing a black and yellow Steeler's jacket stumbled by and pitched into the elevator door. "Wasshh out! Idiots!" He teetered forward like he was about to fall over onto them.

Another guy, short and stocky, stepped in and pushed the drunk away. "Easy there, big guy."

The Steeler's fan eyeballed him for a second, drunkenly calculating the odds of who would end up with the beat down, and then lurched away. "Schtay outta my waayy."

The stocky guy turned to check on them. "You okay?"

Lily was about to thank him when a high-pitched whine stole her attention.

"What is that?" someone said.

Lily pulled Piper over and they peered through the wires.

It was coming from their right, getting louder and louder. Everyone on the observation deck, except for the obnoxiously drunk idiot, stared in that direction to see what it was.

It came out of nowhere.

It wasn't there one second and was the next.

Glints of moonlight revealed an enormous jet airliner streaking toward them down the strip. A wing clipped a building and the shriek of metal was soon followed by an enormous explosion when it hit the ground. A blinding fireball rose into the sky, lighting up the strip like it was day. Roiling yellow flames rose in a column into the sky. A wave of heat washed over them. Fires ignited as jet fuel and sparks combined in devastating fashion. One of the plane's jet engines tumbled down the street, took a big bounce and then landed in the Bellagio fountains. It splashed and rolled to a stop, flames licking off the top and steam hissing.

The brilliance of the expanding fireball in the sky faded as it cooled into black smoke. Already a caustic scent floated their way.

"Oh my God," someone said.

A jolt of fear punched Lily right in the stomach. Her dad was flying home that night.

Did his plane go down just like that one?

6

Lily pushed the thought away. Knowing what could've happened but not knowing what did happen was only going to make her crazy. She didn't have time for that right now.

No, she had to put that away for now and focus on getting out of this cage. She found the stocky guy on the other side of the viewing platform, staring out at a large fire to the south. Likely where the airport was. "Excuse me," she said as she tapped his shoulder.

He turned and forced a thin smile. "Hey."

"Thanks for backing that guy off."

He shrugged. "No prob. My old man was a mean drunk. Always hated it."

"Can I ask for your help?"

"Sure. Is he bothering you again?"

"No, not that. It's the elevator doors. I need to get them open."

"What? Why?"

"There's a maintenance ladder inside that my friend and I are going to take down."

"Really? Why not just wait for them to come get us?"

Lily chewed her lip. She didn't want to go into it and she definitely didn't want to start a panic with a dozen strangers in the enclosed space. "Look around. Any available response is going to go to putting out those fires and helping people injured in car crashes. They're going to have higher priorities than us."

"We're a long way up," he said.

"Don't remind me," she said, half-heartedly trying to inject a little humor.

"You sure?"

She nodded.

"Okay."

"Thanks." Lily rejoined Piper and dug into her pack. She pulled out a hinged rod about eight inches long.

"What's that?" Piper said.

Holding it horizontal, Lily showed how the hinge

allowed the last third of the rod to drop to vertical. "It's an elevator drop key. It's nearly impossible to get modern elevator doors open without one."

"And why do you have it in your bag?"

Lily flashed her a *you know why* look.

"Oh, right."

Lily's dad had been adamant that she add it to her backpack since she was going to a city filled with skyscrapers. She'd made such a big stink about how ridiculous he was being because it had seemed ridiculous at the time. And yet, here she was using it.

She found the tiny hole in the door up near the top and inserted the rod. The hinged part went through and the end clunked down. She fiddled with it for a second until it engaged. A turn of the key and the safety mechanism disengaged.

With Lily and Piper pulling on one side and the stocky guy on the other, they wrenched the doors open a couple of feet.

Lily strapped on the headlamp and looked over the edge.

It was a long way down. She'd gone climbing with Colton quite a few times while they were together. He was an adrenaline junkie that always liked to push the envelope. So the height didn't bother her much. Then again, she didn't have a climbing harness, ropes and all the usual gear.

She turned to Piper. "We're going to be fine."

Piper's lips pressed into a tight line and she nodded.

Lily fashioned and secured a makeshift harness around Piper's thighs and torso. She'd never done anything like it before and so did her best. She secured the other end around her waist and shoulders, giving the doubled-over cord that connected them six to seven feet of play. She secured it with a figure-eight follow through knot ended with a double fisherman's knot for extra safety.

For whatever that was worth.

"Alright, you're going first and I'll be right behind you. Go slow and whatever you do, don't look down. It's just a ladder." She glanced at Piper's feet. "Take off the stripper heels." She stuffed them into her pack and they were ready.

"Whaashoo guyshh doing?"

The drunk idiot again.

Their stocky friend stepped between them with his hands raised. "You need to back up, man."

"Shhcrew you!" the drunk took a wild swing as the other guy ducked to the side. The drunk guy's momentum pulled him forward toward the open elevator doors.

Lily grabbed for his arm and got a hold of it.

The stocky guy wrapped an arm around his waist and shoved him away. The drunk squared up like the fight was on but then turned, mumbling threats and promises of what would happen next.

Lily found the plastic water bottle in her pack and handed it over to their helper. "Don't wait too long."

He accepted it with a nod of thanks. "Be careful."

"You too." Lily secured the headlamp to Piper's head so she would have the best light possible. "Keep your eyes on the ladder and don't let go with your hands until a foot is solidly on the next rung. Understand?"

Piper nodded, but she was trembling with fear.

Lily wanted to hug her, tell her she loved her and that they'd be best friends forever. But she didn't because then they'd both break down crying and totally fall apart.

Piper reached into the elevator shaft and got onto the ladder. Lily played out the paracord and then followed her out.

The metal rungs were still warm from the afternoon heat.

"Good luck."

She looked up. "We'll tell someone at the hotel that you're up here and need help."

"Thanks."

The play in the cord drew taut so Lily started down, matching Piper's pace to manage the tautness of the length between them. If Piper did slip, she wanted to stop the fall immediately. Any extra play would cause the cord to snap and that might sever it or yank her off the ladder.

Either outcome would be worst case scenario.

Slow and steady, they descended down the ladder. Lily knew something terrible would happen. Some small misstep where it all went wrong. Every second felt like it could be the last.

But they kept going.

And she nearly kicked Piper in the head before she realized they'd made it. She climbed down next to Piper in a small space next to the elevator car. They fell into each other's arms.

Piper cried and laughed and a gob of snot shot out of her nose into Lily's hair.

"Ewww!"

"Sorry," Piper said as she tried to rake it out.

Lily yelled up the shaft. "We made it!"

A round of cheers and excited shouting echoed back.

She untied and gathered up the paracord. She'd found uses for it now and again, but nothing like this. Nothing life or death. But she'd had it when it counted. Her dad was right.

Ninety-nine percent of the time, you didn't need this or that and life went on like normal and it was no problem.

But that one percent was real.

And in those situations, being prepared could make all the difference.

She was just starting to understand exactly what that meant.

7

They exited the maintenance door into a cavern-like lobby hidden in shadows. One corner of the tower's base extended down from the ceiling and into the floor. Lily's headlamp swept over what appeared to be a quaint village somewhere in the hills of France. There were little houses with steep shingled roofs and lattice windows. Hand-painted signs hanging from curled wrought iron fixtures above each store. A faux cobblestone lane wound through the middle.

It was quintessential Las Vegas.

An appealing fabrication. An attractive exterior with little substance underneath.

Lily glanced down at Piper's bare feet. With all the debris scattered around, it was asking for trouble. She dug out one of Piper's shoes and lined it up with the edge of the door.

"What are you doing?" Piper said in an alarmed voice.

"I'm breaking off the stripper heel."

Piper snatched it away. "You most definitely are not! And they are not stripper heels! They're fake Jimmy Choo's!"

"Piper, what if we have to run? Can you run in heels like that?"

She slipped it on and held out a demanding hand. "Give me the other one!"

Against her better judgement, Lily turned it over.

Piper put it on and walked in a little circle. "I can move just fine, thank you very much."

Lily decided to let it go. It would sort itself out. She just hoped that it didn't cause a big problem when it did. "Come on," she said as she tugged Piper's elbow and headed in the direction of the reception area. They threaded through a section of slot machines, turned down a row, and Lily yelped with surprise.

An old man sat in front of a slot machine. He was slumped down in the chair with his chin on his chest. A ring of thin silver hair surrounded a bald spot on top of his head. The light reflected off the mottled, bare skin.

How had he died?

Maybe a heart attack or a stroke or something. Her dad said that the frail and infirm were going to be hit hard by the unfolding calamity. Those least able to endure the difficulties would fall first.

It was only the second dead body she'd ever seen in person. The first was Grandpa's funeral. Even with all the makeup, he'd still looked so dull, so empty. That was when she knew it wasn't him. Not anymore. The spark that was Grandpa had left. She'd broken down crying then. Not because of the body.

It was discarded baggage.

She'd wept for the spark that would never light up her life again.

Lily turned sideways to edge by the body, when a hand shot out and grasped her arm. She jumped back and ripped her arm free.

He was definitely not dead!

"This is my row! Don't even think about it!"

The fumes rolling off him nearly singed her nose hairs.

"What?" she said.

"One of these babies is about to pay out big time," he said as he squinted at her with suspicion. "And no one is going to steal it from me."

"We don't want your machines."

He eyed them for a second, deciding if he believed them or not. He must've because he nodded. His eyes ran down Piper's dress, long legs and stopped at her heels. "You a stripper?"

Piper made a shocked face like she couldn't believe he'd just said that. It must've been a put on because Lily had already basically said the same thing.

Lily considered saying I told you so, but thought better of it. "Do you, uh, need help?" she asked.

He grabbed a glass, finished whatever it was, and shoved it at her. "Another gin and tonic to wet my whistle."

"Sorry, we don't work here."

He snorted grumpily. "Well, tell someone to turn the lights back on and get me another drink. And tell them I won't be fooled into giving up right when I'm about to hit the jackpot." He turned back toward the machine in front of him. "They're always pulling some shenanigans trying to keep you from winning what's yours."

"Okay, we'll tell them." Lily shot Piper a look and the two scooted by.

Once they were out of earshot, Piper whispered, "That guy's in for a rude awakening when he finally sobers up. If he ever sobers up."

They kept going and Lily struggled to stay calm. It was just so creepy. Earlier, there had been hundreds of people filling the casino, restaurants and stores. Now, it was a ghost town.

Something crashed nearby and they froze to see what.

A couple of guys not much older than them stood in front of a broken window. A jewelry store with necklaces, watches and earrings in the display window. They glanced over when Lily's light hit them, turning to shine their own lights back. "You looking for trouble?" the larger one said as he tapped a tire iron against the wall. The other snatched up the items within reach, before climbing through the shattered pane.

"No," Lily croaked as she and Piper backed away. They turned and ran in the other direction and thankfully heard no signs of pursuit.

People were looting already?

On the one hand, she could hardly believe it. On the other, it made sense. Criminals broke the law even when things were functioning and the threat of getting caught was very real. Now that that barrier had been removed, they would be the first to take advantage.

They hurried around another corner before slowing to a walk, panting more from fear than exhaustion. They turned in a circle, the headlamp's disc of illumination sliding over surfaces. She didn't recognize anything.

They made these places like mazes. Unless you had a map or had been there a few times, it was easy to get lost. Lily was trying to decide where to go next when someone shouted.

"Stop!"

A bright beam landed on them.

Before she could react, the man was next to them, bouncing the light back and forth.

"What are you two doing?"

Lily noticed with relief the badge on his chest. Casino security. He kept the flashlight trained on them while his other hand rested on the grip of the pistol holstered at his hip.

"We were in the Eiffel Tower when the power cut off," Lily said, nervously glancing at the hand on the pistol.

He wouldn't shoot them? Would he?

"How did you get down?"

"We got the doors open and climbed down the maintenance ladder."

His eyes widened with surprise. "That's a long way."

Piper snorted. "Yeah, and it was terrifying."

"Do you have a room here?"

"No, we're at Mandalay Bay," Piper said. "I love the aquariums."

The guy shot her a look like she was crazy. "Well, you can't be in here. This area is closed until further notice." He stepped to the side and gestured. "I'll escort you to the exit."

"Okay," Lily said, even though the thought of going out into the street was anything but okay. "There are people still trapped at the top of the tower. They need help."

"We're overwhelmed right now so they're going to have to sit tight. But thanks for letting me know."

"Also, there were a couple of guys further back that broke into a jewelry store."

His fleshy cheeks quivered with anger. He grabbed the two-way radio clipped to his belt. "How many?"

"Two."

"Were they armed?"

"One had a tire iron. That's all I saw."

He spoke into the radio. "Nelson, this is Burnett. We've got a break-in at Bocelli's. Confirmed two males. One armed with a tire iron. I'm heading there now and could use backup."

Lily and Piper waited while the guard finished the communication.

"Alright." He pointed off to the right. "Keep going in that direction. You'll pass a creperie place and a few other shops. The exit is a little further on. All the doors are chained shut except for one. Use that one and make sure it latches when you close it. Understood?"

Lily considered telling him about the old man at the slot machine, but decided against it. His next drink would have to wait.

"Yes. Thanks," Lily said as the guard turned to leave.

They followed the directions and stepped out the door.

Lily closed it behind them and heard it click. She tried to pull it open, but the lock had engaged.

They stood in the shadows of a stone archway, staring out at the street and the wide pool of the Bellagio beyond.

And it was nothing like it had been when they'd arrived just hours ago.

Now, it was like a war zone.

And from what her dad had said about the aftermath of an EMP attack, she knew it was going to get much, much worse.

8

Donny Price pulled into a strip mall on the far south end of the Vegas strip.

"We gettin' some Panda Express?" his best and only friend, Zeke Bell, asked from the passenger's seat.

"Hell no. I don't eat that greasy slop. We're going to McDonald's…after."

They went past a liquor store and parked right under the golden arches. He shut off the ignition and the old Chevy El Camino sputtered a few times before going quiet. Across Las Vegas Blvd was their first destination.

Mandalay Bay Resort and Casino.

But it cost twenty dollars to park there and Donny wasn't about to waste a single red cent on parking when he could just as easily park across the street for free.

He patted the pair of fuzzy red dice hanging from the rear view mirror. "Lady Luck is gonna be on my side tonight. I can feel it."

Zeke's leg was going like a jackhammer while he blew a lungful of smoke out the window. After recovering from a bout of coughing, Zeke passed the meth pipe and lighter over. "You said that before, but I don't see us drivin' no Lamborghini."

Donny had the urge, a strong one, to punch his friend in the ear for talking trash on the Mino. "Shut your mouth. You don't know nothin'." He sparked up and inhaled deeply, the sharp smoke filled his chest and the tingles of the oncoming high rolled in. He went through his own spell of hacking coughs and came out the other side all the better.

The speed was doing its thing. Filling his limbs with a thousand volts of electric satisfaction.

That was the good news.

The bad news was that they'd just smoked up the last of it. The even worse news was that there was no chance Jax was going to front him any more without first settling up on his debt.

Donny ran a fingertip along a five-inch slice in the dashboard.

The Mino had a lot of scars and every one told a story. That one told the story of when a hooker tried to rip him off by taking his money and trying to bolt. All he'd wanted was what he paid for and so that was what he took. Of course, that was after she drew a knife on him and a wild swing missed his face by inches and instead made that cut. After he was finished getting his money's worth, he even paid her.

Just because it was the gentlemanly thing to do.

It wouldn't have taken much to repair it, but he liked that story and it gave the Mino more character.

Donny tucked the pipe up under the console in the secret spot he'd found that cops never could. He dropped the lighter in his shirt pocket and flicked the dice, feeling the rush jagging through his veins.

"Man, you sure about this?" Zeke asked. "I mean, what if you don't win? Jax doesn't bluff. He'll kill you and probably me too just to send a message."

Donny spat a glob of thick spit out the window. "I ain't afraid of him." He reached under the seat and pulled out a pistol. "He's the one that should be afraid."

Even as he said it, he knew it was nothing but talk. Everyone was afraid of Jackson Cook. He ran drugs and whores and stolen goods and, unlike most of the other guys that had climbed up the chain of criminal enterprise, he never turned civilized. He never got soft.

No, he enjoyed personally enforcing the rules from time to time. It kept him in touch with his roots, he liked to say. With him, that meant torture and eventually a bullet to the brain.

Eventually.

Which was why Donny was very nervous indeed about owing him thirteen hundred dollars. The debt had started small. Nothing to worry about. But he never stopped needing the next fix and he couldn't always pay for it up front. So he ended up scoring more on credit. Again and again.

Jax loved selling on credit because then he had his claws in you. And that meant he could slowly bleed you dry. Take everything before he was finished.

But Donny was about to change all that. He dug a wad of crumpled bills out of his pocket. Nine hundred dollars. Hard-earned dollars too. The details were blurry from tweaking so hard, but this bankroll was the result of a string of successful convenience store robberies. That was high risk work. You never knew when one of those dumbshit clerks would pull a gun like they were some kind of Dirty Harry out for justice.

He hadn't killed anyone, but he would've if it had come to that. It was nothing personal. It was just what it was. Jax was going to kill him if he didn't come up with the cash. It wasn't like Donny had some fancy college degree and a good-paying job. He did what he had to do to get by. That's always how it had been, so far.

But he was meant for something bigger and better. He just had to survive long enough to get there. And that meant settling his debt with Jax. Sure, he could knock a chunk off the debt by turning over his bankroll and maybe that would buy him time.

But for how long?

And for what? He'd be dead broke again and still owe $400 that was racking up interest every single day it went unpaid.

Nope.

That wouldn't change anything. He had to win big and get out from under it once and for all. And then he'd never buy from that psychopath again.

Donny breathed in the handful of cash. Smelled like cocaine and a hooker's panties after a long night on the job. He remembered watching a show on TV that said ninety percent of paper money had traces of cocaine and poop on it. Sounded about right considering what he'd seen.

He stared at the bills a second and another crazy thought hit him. The crank sometimes worked like that.

People would do anything to get more of these rectangular pieces of green paper. They'd cheat. They'd lie. They'd steal. Hell, he knew a few losers that would kill their own grandmothers for less than he had here.

For nothing but a piece of paper.

It didn't fill your belly or quench your thirst and even get you high.

He chuckled to himself, knowing the truth of it. The truth was that these green pieces of paper could get you all those other things. Anything you wanted. Cash was king and everything else served at its beck and call.

"What're you laughing about?" Zeke said.

Donny glanced over and noticed the glazed look in Zeke's eyes. He knew his were the same. "Nothin'. You ready?"

"Sure."

Donny checked himself in the mirror. He raked a hand through greasy black hair and smiled, revealing a mouth full of yellowed, rotting teeth. The ones that were still there anyway. Meth did a number on teeth and his were a textbook case. He snapped his mouth shut and slapped the mirror away. It didn't matter. He'd be rich enough to get them all replaced someday.

He leaned forward and kissed the fuzzy red dice. He sent up a silent prayer to Lady Luck, begging her to treat him right for just one damn time in his cursed life.

Because if she did her usual thing tonight, he was very much a dead man.

9

They strolled through the front entrance of the Mandalay Bay Resort and Casino probably looking just like those guys in Ocean's Eleven. All suave, in charge and ready to take the bull by the horns.

That's the way it felt to Donny, anyway.

They made a beeline for the casino floor which wasn't hard to find on account of all the flashing lights, bing bong noises and cloud of cigarette smoke.

More than a few heads turned as they made their way through. Zeke picked at the stains on his shirt. He was always so worried about everything.

Donny punched him in the shoulder. "Relax, man. We're not here to stick up the joint. We're paying customers. This place exists to serve us."

Zeke made like he was cool but it wasn't convincing. That was okay. He was along for the ride.

Tonight was all about Donny's destiny. This would be the start of something bigger and better.

He found the cashier, exchanged his nine hundred dollars for chips and got free passes to the shark reef aquarium, drink vouchers, and a couple of buffet vouchers. He flashed them in Zeke's face. "And you wanted Panda Express. Pffft." He pocketed the chips, all heady again about how he was trading one essentially meaningless form of wealth for another and how it was still as good as gold, so long as everybody kept on agreeing that it was.

They got directions to the roulette tables and headed over. They threaded through a maze of blackjack tables and arrived in the promised land. They plopped down in a couple of empty chairs, next to a young couple that were drunk as skunks and pawing all over each other. They were in town for a wild weekend. Locals didn't act like that. Tourists often went home filled with regret after losing a wad of cash and picking up a permanent infection.

What happened in Vegas didn't always stay in Vegas.

Donny was different. This was his city. He was here to stay.

He touched the blue felt covering the table and his fingertips sizzled with possibility. Sure, that could've been the speed talking, but whatever. He felt it and it was real. This was where his horrible, tragic, pathetic life was finally going to take a turn for the better.

He pulled out all the chips and stacked them up in piles. That got the attention of a few of the other players at the table. Not the couple though. If they kept it up like that, he was gonna have to suggest they get a room. She was hot and it was too much of a distraction.

Zeke sat next to him, his leg still bouncing like he was tapping out a telegraph message.

Donny flagged down a passing waitress and ordered a couple of whiskies neat. No chance he was going to let them fill it up with anything else. Booze did a good job of softening the sharp edges of being cranked up.

"Gimme a smoke," he said as he reached out a hand. Zeke hooked them both up and soon they had a swirling cloud drifting away above their heads. The drinks arrived and he handed over a couple of vouchers. He winked as she waited for a tip.

She finally gave up and huffed away.

Her anger was like tipping him. He grinned and enjoyed the moment.

They watched the wheel spin and the ball drop. Bets won and lost as they sipped on the whisky and burned through a few cigarettes.

No sense rushing fate.

It would be there, waiting for him when he was ready.

They finally finished their drinks and stubbed cigarette butts out in the bottom of the empty glasses.

Donny stared at the wheel and finally let the question come into his mind that he'd purposefully avoided so far.

Red or Black?

Sure, he could've put it all on a number and gotten a huge payout if it turned up. But what were the odds of that happening? He didn't know, but they weren't good.

Red or black was simple. And the odds were fifty-fifty except for the zeros on the wheel. He took a single chip and moved his hand toward the red diamond and then the black, testing to see if maybe one felt different than the other.

But no, they felt the same. Cool and quiet and giving away no secrets.

He closed his eyes and tried to listen for Lady Luck's voice, anything really that might tell him which color the steel ball would land on next.

Damn it. Still nothing.

Well, he couldn't sit here all night waiting for a sign that might never come. He wrapped his hands around the stacks of chips, took a deep breath, and slid them over to red.

His heart rate spiked as others at the table chattered about the ballsy bet. They didn't know the half of it. His life was on the table.

The man was about to call an end to betting when something struck Donny in the chest. A flash that maybe was the speed or maybe something else. Without thinking, he shoved the chips over to black and the man waved off any more betting.

The wheel blurred and the ball circled around in the opposite direction.

This was it!

All or nothing!

Was he wrong to move to black?

Did he just screw himself and it was gonna end up going red?

Oh God, had he just killed himself with that move?

The wheel slowed and the silver ball jumped and skipped around. It hit the edges of various numbered slots, bouncing back and forth as it slowed.

It bounced into a red slot and Donny nearly screamed as it looked like it would stay there.

Then, it took one last hop and landed on black.

And stayed there.

Donny whooped with joy. He leaped out of his seat and accidentally smacked the slobber swapping guy in the back of the head. He jumped up and down, hollering incoherently while dragging Zeke up to join him in a celebratory dance that had no particular rhythm or steps.

"Black wins," the man said. He counted out nine hundred dollars worth of poker chips and slid them over.

Donny slapped the table so hard he winced. Still, the pain was nothing compared to the joy of winning. He now had eighteen hundred dollars!

Eighteen hundred!

He could pay off Jax, get an eight ball to celebrate and he'd still have money in his pocket!

He scooped up all the chips and was about to

toss one to the guy working the table. But he stuffed them all into his bulging pockets because he needed it more. He wrapped an arm around Zeke. "Times they are a changing, my friend. Did I tell you or did I tell you?"

Zeke laughed and the two headed over to cash out.

Donny stacked up all the chips on the counter and grinned at the lady who'd not so long ago set him up with the first nine hundred.

"Looks like someone's had a good night," she said as she counted through them.

"Oh yeah," Donny said, being sure to keep a close eye on her. He wasn't about to get cheated after doing all the hard work to get this far.

She finished the count. "One thousand eight hundred dollars. How would you like that?"

"Cold, hard cash, baby," he replied, barely able to contain his joy.

She nodded and tapped away on a computer screen to finish the transaction.

Donny pulled Zeke into a headlock and squeezed. "We're going places, amigo. Stick with me and the sky is the limit!"

And then the lights throughout the casino cut off.

10

"What the hell?" Donny said as he looked around, tried to look around, rather, because the whole place was as dark as the inside of a closet.

"Donny, you there?" Zeke said, his voice faltering.

"Of course I'm here, you idiot."

Glasses shattered and chairs and people crashed to the floor. Some lady screamed, "My purse! Someone took my purse!"

An angry, deep voice bellowed, "Turn the damn lights back on!"

More shouting followed until it was hard to make out what any particular one was saying.

The place was going crazy.

A heavier thud to his left that sounded like a

gambling table got thrown over. The plastic clinking of an avalanche of poker chips. Donny had half a mind to get over there and scoop up as many of them as he could before the lights came back on and the opportunity ended.

But no.

He wanted his money first.

He reached out in the dark and his finger smacked into the edge of the counter. "Oww." He'd misjudged it and probably jammed a knuckle. He continued forward until he found the cashier's arm. "Lady, give me my eighteen hundred dollars."

She tried to pull away, but he held tight. "Umm, sir, wait just a minute."

Flashlights clicked on here and there as security guards got their act together. One of the beams lit up a blackjack table and revealed some frat boy wearing a green fraternity jacket scooping chips off the table. He froze when he realized he was no longer in the dark. A biker looking guy in a black leather jacket next to him saw what was happening and didn't take it kindly. Must've been his chips. He jumped on the kid and started wailing on him. Blood exploded from the frat boy's nose and the punches kept dropping as a security guard moved in to break it up.

Strong hands grasped Donny's hand and tore it

loose. He turned back to get blinded by a flashlight and then howled with pain as a metal gate crashed down on his forearm. He yanked it back and the gate came down again and clicked shut.

A huge guard stood behind the cashier lady. He raked a flashlight over the people working inside the cage. "Secure the cashier windows!" Metal scraped and clanged as the other gates dropped and locked shut.

Donny banged on the bars with his good hand. "Hey! I need my money! Give me my money!"

The flashlight bounced to his face, blinding him again. "All transactions are temporarily suspended."

Anger welled up in Donny's chest. It wanted to come out and hurt someone. He pounded on the bars that separated him from his money. "Suspended, my ass! You owe me eighteen hundred dollars and I want it now!"

"Back away from the window, sir!" the guard ordered as his free hand went to the pistol holstered at his hip.

Donny couldn't believe it. He'd won fair and square and the idiot was threatening to shoot him for wanting his money? If they thought he was leaving without it, they had another thing coming. Fury burned through his veins. He grabbed the bars with both hands and tried to tear them down. "Give me my money or I will get in there and break your skull in half!"

"Donny!" Zeke shouted, too late.

Someone grabbed him from behind and twisted an arm behind his back. Before he knew it, both arms were wrenched together and a zip tie was pulled tight around his wrists.

He got spun around and frog-marched away. Another guard was doing the same to Zeke. The guards dragged them to the exit and then threw them outside.

Donny tripped and didn't have his hands free to catch himself. So he fell forward and hit the pavement face first. His face bounced off the hard surface and an already-loose tooth broke free in his mouth. Blood poured out of a busted lip as he rolled onto his back. He spat the tooth out along with a lot of blood. "I will kill you for this! I will kill you all!"

The guards didn't hear because they'd already gone back inside and locked the door.

Donny strained to get his hands free but that only made the ties cut painfully into his wrists.

Zeke appeared at his side, hooked an arm under him and pulled him up. He used a pocket knife to cut him loose.

Donny stumbled to the side and Zeke grabbed him before he fell over. "You okay, man?"

Donny jerked away. "Let go of me!" He touched his lip and winced. He glared at the entrance to the casino. A hundred violent thoughts swirled in his mind.

Did they think he was gonna take this lying down? Did they honestly believe they could steal his money and that would be the end of it?

He spat out some blood, then swiped at more dribbling down his chin. He turned to Zeke and caught the confused look in the pale light.

There was nothing to be confused about.

It was simple, actually.

He grabbed Zeke by the collar and twisted his shirt up in a clenched fist. "We're getting my money, one way or another."

11

Samantha Bowman opened the rear door of the silver Crew Cab F150. Cade's pride and joy, as he'd so often reminded her during his time away. It was a decade old but looked basically new. Objectively, she could see it was a nice vehicle, but that kind of thing never did much for her.

She wasn't into cars. Her old Volvo was proof of that. That thing was showing its age. What had once been a glossy brown that she'd personally found quite pleasing had long ago faded into a dull beige. The hydraulic shocks that held the back hatch up died years ago. She used a dowel rod instead. They'd been meaning to fix it for years, but there was always a higher priority that ended up needing the money.

Besides, a dowel rod did the trick so the shocks didn't technically need to be replaced.

Growing up without much money, she'd been forced to be thrifty by necessity. She'd lived in Durango, Colorado her entire forty-four years and had witnessed the sweeping changes roll through. Some for the better. It had been much poorer when she was young, but the influx of tourism and people had changed that over the years. Nearly twenty thousand people now called it home. Double what it was when she was born.

In some ways, it felt nothing like the small town she remembered from her youth. There'd never been rush hour traffic back then. The farmers markets never featured things like artisanal butter or limited run beer crafted at a local microbrewery.

She pulled out bags of groceries and set them on the driveway.

"Evening, Sam," a voice said.

She went by Sam instead of Samantha. She'd endured a lot of teasing for having a boy's name when she was young. But there had been no going back after she found out her mother named her after a cheesy sixties sitcom about a witch that was a housewife. Her mother's favorite show of all time.

She'd gone by Sam ever since. The only one that

called her Samantha with unerring regularity was her mother. And it still drove her crazy.

Sam turned to see Gary Hensley, the next door neighbor, waving from the front porch chair he habitually occupied ever since he retired a few years ago. He hadn't retired by choice either, as he would tell anyone whether they asked or not. The post office in town had forced him into early retirement and he was still bitter about it.

"Need a hand with that?"

She smiled. As much as Durango had changed over the years, some things had stayed the same. Like knowing the neighbors and looking out for each other.

"Ethan was supposed to meet me out here to help, but it looks like that fell through."

Gary shook his head as he marched over. He didn't walk so much as march everywhere he went. He said it was on account of his years in the Marine Corps. He was fond of saying that he left the corps to become a civilian and make some real money, but the corps never left him. And then he became a career postal worker. So he never got rich, but the benefits were good.

He grabbed up all but one bag, a token gesture to indicate that while he believed in chivalry, he didn't think women were any less capable of doing things.

Most things.

But they'd agreed not to talk about that again after getting into it the last time.

"Kids these days have their heads buried in those *video games*." He said the last part like it was something no normal person could ever understand.

"Tell me about it," she replied as she shut the door. She scooped up the remaining bag and headed for the front door of their split-level ranch style house. They'd followed the advice that every well-meaning friend and commission-seeking real estate agent advocated.

Buy the biggest house you can afford. Stretch a little if you have to. You'll regret it later if you don't.

And all those people were right until they weren't. Until that housing crisis came along and the economy took a nose dive. Even after the talking head pundits on the news declared the economy recovered and America to be flourishing once again, their personal finances had never fully recovered.

Between the cost of living constantly climbing higher and construction in the local area slowing down, the last year hadn't been easy. And that was before adding the cost of a retirement home for her mother. Her job as a fifth grade teacher at Riverview Elementary kept them insured but didn't pay much. Which was why her husband had spent the last two months in Seattle working a lucrative short-term job to make ends meet. Neither of them were happy about it, but they'd survived and now he was coming home.

Finally.

She opened the front door and Dennis charged out, his tail wagging so hard it swung his rear back and forth. He was a sixty pound brindle Boxer that they'd adopted from a local rescue organization. He bounced around, licking her hands, begging for attention.

She stroked his head to calm him down because otherwise he'd go on like this forever. She stepped aside so Gary could go in with all the bags.

He smiled, "Please, after you."

She considered for half a second making a thing of it. It was only reasonable that he should go first because he had most of the bags and he was helping her, after all. But then she decided against it. She was too tired and besides, he was just being nice. She waved the dog inside and followed.

Apparently satisfied with her greeting, Dennis buzzed around Gary, sniffing at the grocery bags.

"Hey, big guy," Gary said in the softer tone that she'd only ever heard him use with animals. "Keeping an eye on things, right?"

Dennis barked and circled around as they trod the well-worn path in the linoleum floor to the kitchen.

"You really should keep the door locked when you're not home."

How many times had her husband said the same thing? Especially after the recent spate of burglaries in the adjacent trailer park.

"Ethan's home."

Gary snorted. "A herd of elephants could trample through your living room and that kid wouldn't hear."

Samantha bristled for an instant. She had no problem pointing out every single one of her son's flaws, but another person doing it was another matter entirely. It brought out the mama bear in her.

"Ethan! Ethan!" she yelled, to no avail. She didn't have to go up the half-flight of stairs to his room to know why he wasn't responding.

Gary set the bags on the laminated countertop, spreading them out and testing each to make sure none fell over. "Did you hear there's been another break-in?"

Another?

How many was that in the last couple of months? Three? Four?

"No. I've been a little out the loop since Cade's been away."

"Yep, the Donovans at the end of the street."

The Donovans lived in the first house on Hidden Valley Circle and so were closest to the trailer park next door. Samantha didn't like to make judgements about trailer parks and white trash and all that because there were plenty of trailer parks that were just fine and filled with good people.

But that particular one had been going down hill for a long time. She'd seen some questionable characters walking the streets after dark any number of times.

Gary scratched Dennis behind the ear and then started unpacking the bags, even though she hadn't asked him to. "You folks ever get that DIY alarm system installed?"

"Haven't gotten around to it yet. It's on a long list of To Dos for Cade."

"He's supposed to be coming back any day now, right?"

She nodded as a little jolt of anticipation zapped her in the chest. Eight weeks was too long to be away. But like anyone else, they did what they had to do. "He's coming back tonight."

Gary plucked out a bottle of champagne, eyeing it before setting it on the counter.

Samantha saw him pull a face, but ignored it. Yes, she'd bought champagne to celebrate her husband coming home. She'd even bought a new black lace nightie. One that she was proud to say looked pretty damn good on her, despite the dreaded forty-five being right around the corner. Staying in shape had always been important to her. She walked Dennis several times a week and even got a spin class in most weekends. The exercise wasn't the hard part.

The not gorging on chocolate was.

It was just so delicious and it always delivered.

Tonight was special. Her husband was coming home. Chocolate and champagne were definitely on the menu.

"Well," Gary said as he stuffed the empty bags into one, "tell him I said welcome back and that I haven't forgotten about my post-hole digger."

Sam laughed out loud. Cade and Gary had a long history of borrowing tools back and forth. It was all good-natured and she was pretty sure they enjoyed having something loaned out just so they could mention it from time to time. "Thanks for the help, Gary."

"No problem at all." He snapped off a nod like a salute, gave a few more scratches to Dennis, and then headed for the front door.

She heard it shut and reached for her phone. Cade should be landing in San Francisco soon. Which meant he'd be on a flight to the local airport soon after and then in her arms not long after that.

Which reminded her, she needed a shower. Bad.

"Ethan!"

Still nothing.

Had Dennis been fed? She glanced at his food bowl but that wasn't helpful because it was always spotless. His tongue left it cleaner than a dishwasher, not counting all the slobber germs.

God help that kid if he was bleary-eyed from playing video games and hadn't finished his homework and fed the dog. She'd lock his gaming console up for a week and let him stew on it. But she'd deal with that headache in a minute. First, she wanted to text Cade.

Call me when you can. Love you.

He texted back.

Will do. Love you too.

He must've arrived early. Probably taxiing to the arrival gate. He was finally coming home.

She thought of what would be their first night together in forever and decided to add a teaser. He was going to be exhausted, but she was confident she could get him properly motivated.

Champagne and a sexy black nightie await. Hope you're—

The kitchen and living room lights went dark.

12

Her fingers froze above the phone screen.

Had the main breaker tripped for some reason?

She looked out the kitchen window and saw that the neighbor's two-story house opposite the backyard was also dark. And their house was never dark. They left every light on pretty much all the time, including the back patio floodlights. Floodlights that lit up both of their backyards like it was day. Cade had gone over to talk to them about it once or twice. They didn't act like jerks. They'd apologized and it had gotten better for a week or two.

But then it went back to normal.

All the lights, all the time.

But now?

Their house was pitch black.

So it was another power outage. They'd had a couple last winter after big snow storms took out transmission lines.

But it was June so snow wasn't the problem. It had been pretty windy that day so maybe that was it.

Whatever it was, hopefully the power would come back on soon. If not, she'd have to pull the portable generator out of the garage to keep the groceries from going bad. Fortunately, it wouldn't be too much of a hassle because they already had a system for using it and Cade religiously checked it each season to ensure it would work when needed.

She finished the text.

—not too tired for the welcome I have in mind...

She considered not sending it, figuring it would come off sounding stupid and be more likely to make him laugh than get him hot under the collar.

Whatever. She missed his presence in their bed. The snuggles and his heat that seeped into her bones and made her fall right to sleep. And after eight long weeks, she also missed being intimate.

She hit send and was about to put down the phone when it bounced back as undelivered. She tried again and got the same result. Then she noticed that there was no network signal. She flicked on wifi and waited for it to connect to the house's network.

Nothing.

But that made sense. The outage would've shut off the modem and router.

"Mom!" Ethan yelled as he slid into the kitchen. Socks on linoleum did that.

On the first night they stayed in the house, Cade had done a remarkable Tom Cruise in the movie Risky Business. Floor sliding, long sleeve shirt with the upturned collar, tightie whities, white socks, singing into a candlestick holder. The whole bit. And she'd laughed until her sides hurt.

"Mom, what happened to the electricity?" He shined his headlamp in her eyes and she waved it away.

"It's just a power outage. Relax."

"Just a power outage? Mom, Wyatt and I were about to kill the Platinum Astral Demigorgon! Do you have any idea how many XP that's worth?"

She shook her head. She didn't. She had no idea what XP were, much less how many killing a whatever he said was worth.

He paced back and forth, frantic with worry. Awkwardly long arms and legs making him vaguely tree like. At fourteen years old, he'd sprouted like a weed but had yet to fill out any of that length. "Oh my god, oh my god, oh my god. What if it didn't save our progress? What if we have to start the Blood Scrolls quest over from the beginning?" He stopped and faced her. "What if we have to start the Blood Scrolls quest completely over?"

She shrugged. "You… have to start it over?"

"You don't get it, mom. It took weeks for us to get this far. Weeks!" He threw his hands up.

"Ethan, pull it together. The power will be back on sooner or later. Whatever you were doing was probably saved. And if not, maybe think of it as good lesson that spending so many hours playing video games is just a waste of time."

He glared at her and spun away to leave.

"Stop!"

He stopped.

"Have you fed Dennis?"

He grinned triumphantly. "Yes!" He turned to leave.

"Stop!"

He stopped.

"And your homework?"

"Yes." Less certain this time.

"All of it?"

He turned back around, eyes glued to the floor. "I

still need to study for the Geography test on Monday."

"And you were playing video games instead? How many times have I told you—"

"I basically know it all already. I just need to review a couple things is all."

"Unbelievable." She pointed in the general direction of the stairs and his room. "Study! Now! And you've lost your Playstation for the weekend."

"The whole weekend? That's not fair!"

"Go! Now! Before I make it longer!"

He was about to protest further, but clamped his mouth shut and left. Not before shooting her a look though.

He'd perfected *the look*. The one that said so many things at once. I hate you. You're so unfair. You're an evil tyrant. I'm going to call Child Protective Services on you.

Yeah, that look.

He must've learned it from his big sister. At eighteen and fourteen, one was maybe starting to leave the irritatingly rebellious stage while the other was ramping up.

Sam blew out a steadying breath. They were both good kids. Usually. It was just tough sometimes. Even more so with their father gone.

She used the light on her phone to head out to the front yard to get a better look. Hidden Valley Circle was on a hill on the west side of town. From the front yard, they could see a broad stretch of Durango below.

She stepped outside and found Gary in his front yard next door having the same idea. "Looks like the outage hit the whole town."

He turned and marched over with a flashlight in hand. "Maybe. Does your phone have service?"

"Uhh, no. I was trying to text Cade and the signal died."

He nodded. "You mind trying something for me?"

"What?"

"Can you try starting your truck?"

She looked at him strangely. "Why?"

"Humor me."

It sounded pointless, but he'd helped her cart in an armload of groceries so she'd go along.

"Be right back," she said as she went inside. She returned with the keys. She unlocked the F150 and climbed in. She inserted the key and cranked the ignition, expecting the throaty engine to rumble to life.

Nothing.

She tried a few more times, but the batteries were dead.

How could that be?

She'd driven it to school and then to the grocery store and it had worked fine. It was bigger than she liked, but Lily and Piper had taken her Volvo to Las Vegas.

She climbed out, perplexed at how it could suddenly have a bad battery. "I don't know what happened. The battery must've died. It was fine all day long."

Gary nodded, a knowing look on his face. .

"What?"

"I know what happened. An *EMP* happened. We've been attacked by a hostile foreign power. Probably North Korea or Iran if we're taking bets."

13

Soaking wet and chilled to the bone, Cade took in the surroundings. A small stretch of sandy beach with a squat white building that looked like one of the old paddlewheel steamboats that used to ply the Mississippi River. A couple of docks extended out into the water to the left. A reproduction of an old pirate ship next to that. The towering silhouettes of a dense cluster of skyscrapers in the distance. A small hill covered in trees to the right.

None of it familiar because he'd never set foot in the city.

And if he wasn't careful, this first visit would be his last.

The pale light of the moon bathed the city in shades of blue and black. Bright orange pockets of fire dotted here and there. More than had been there earlier. A section of the horizon to the south glowing orange.

It took a minute to accept that he was still alive.

And then another to remember that that could change in a heartbeat.

What next?

He needed to get out of the city as soon as possible. San Francisco was a densely populated urban area surrounded on three sides by water. The Golden Gate bridge connected it to the north and the Bay Bridge connected it to the east. There was nothing but ocean to the west and more people and congestion to the south.

The Bay Bridge was his way out.

To where exactly, he didn't know yet.

But he had to get to his daughter. Why did this have to happen when she was stranded in a big city in the middle of the desert?

He silently cursed. The frustration of being so far away and so powerless to help nearly overwhelmed him.

No.

He had to stow that. It wouldn't do any good. And besides, that was the nature of disasters. They didn't wait for it to be a good time to happen. They just happened. And those that survived dealt with the aftermath as best they could.

His teeth chattered and it took focused effort to keep from shaking. First things first. He needed out of these wet clothes.

He turned to find Hudson curled into a ball on his side. "Hey," he said as he touched his shoulder. "You okay?"

The kid uncurled and stared up like he had no idea who he was. His whole body shuddering with the cold or the adrenaline or both.

"Get up. We need to get warm."

Hudson allowed himself to be pulled up.

Cade guided them over to a concrete bench and proceeded to peel off his freezing, clinging clothes. He was yanking his socks off when he glanced over and noticed Hudson sitting there looking miserable.

"Hudson, get out of those clothes. I've got extra."

The kid nodded and followed suit.

Cade dug a headlamp out of his bag and used it to ferret out a set of clothes for each of them. That was it as far as clothes went. The rest of what he'd brought along for the job was in a bag in the plane's cargo compartment at the bottom of the bay.

He finished getting dressed and breathed a sigh of relief when he slipped on the dry sneakers he always kept in his Get Home Bag. Construction boots were great for a job site and backcountry hiking. They were less so for walking long distances. And worse yet walking long distances while soaking wet. He tied his bootlaces together and secured them to the outside of the bag.

"Where do you live?" he asked while Hudson buttoned up a flannel shirt.

"In the Solaire."

He said it like everyone knew what that meant.

"Can you be more specific?"

"Oh, yeah. It's a luxury condo building in the Rincon."

The Rincon?

"How far away is it?"

Hudson pointed toward the grouping of skyscrapers. "Those buildings are the financial district. It's on the other side. A couple of miles from here."

Cade nodded as he considered that.

"What's your name again? Sorry, I don't remember."

"Never told you. It's Cade."

"Cade, thank you." His eyes dropped to his new clothes. "For saving me. For not leaving me behind." He choked up. "For all of this."

"You can buy me a beer later." He finished packing up and slung the bag over his shoulder.

"What did you mean when you said we'd been hit with an EMP?"

The kid had no idea. Which also meant he had no idea of what was coming. The aftermath. The collapse. The carnage to come.

"An EMP is an electromagnetic pulse. It can come from a natural source like a coronal mass ejection or a manufactured source like a nuclear detonation."

"It doesn't look like we've been hit with a nuclear bomb."

"A nuke detonated near ground level causes the kind of damage you're thinking of. An EMP is different. It comes from detonating a nuke high up in the atmosphere. The blast waves don't make it down here."

"Then it's not so bad, right?"

"I wouldn't say that. The resulting gamma rays interact with the upper level atmosphere to create a cascading electromagnetic pulse that destroys anything connected to the grid and a lot of things that use microchips. It's essentially an unimaginably powerful shock."

Hudson chewed on that. "Why do you think it

was an EMP and not a power outage or something else?"

"A few reasons. I was texting my wife and it shut off at the exact same time the lights and everything cut off in the plane. The city went dark as well. Not just the streetlights and buildings and houses. The cars too. All but a few blinked off. No regular power outage could do all that. The only thing I know of that could do that is an EMP. A single nuke detonated two to three hundred miles above Kansas or Nebraska could potentially wipe out the entire country."

"So we're at war?"

"Don't know, but probably."

"Could've been worse, I guess."

"You're not seeing the whole picture. An EMP causes destruction in so many different ways. There are 4000 planes in the air over the continental United States at any given moment. That's around half a million people that just went through some version of an emergency landing. How many landed and how many crashed? I don't know. But you can bet that tens of thousands didn't survive. Maybe hundreds of thousands.

And that's just what's happened in the air. What about traffic on the ground? How many car crashes happened from traffic lights and headlights going dark and people losing control of their vehicles?"

Hudson's jaw dropped open.

"And it's only going to get worse. An EMP kicks a modern society back to the 1800s in an instant."

"What do you mean?"

"Think about it for a second. With the grid down, that means no electricity. People don't realize how much we depend on access to reliable electricity. It's not just about keeping your fridge cold and keeping the lights on. All those high-rises require power to distribute air and water. The vast majority of vehicles made from the early eighties and on use microchips to improve efficiency, comfort and safety. Just like our plane, those vehicles are now toast. That means no more trucks bringing in fuel and food and supplies to a city that absolutely depends on those timely deliveries. What about sanitation? No trucks to make the weekly trash pick up. Between that and a dwindling supply of clean water, it won't take long for an outbreak of cholera or dysentery to hit. I could go on, but you get the idea.

No place is going to have it easy. But big cities are going to fall the fastest."

Cade stopped himself from piling on the doom and gloom. He'd probably already said too much and there was no point pointing out the worst news of all. A congressional commission of experts released an EMP report that spelled out all the different ways that an EMP would wreak havoc on the nation. It concluded that ninety percent of the nation's population would perish in the first year. Ninety percent.

He kept that to himself.

The kid was already holding on by a string. A tattered string, at that.

Hudson's face was slack. He was starting to see the big picture. Then he perked up. "But surely the government will come in and sort it out."

"Not likely. Remember Katrina? That was a regional event and FEMA absolutely failed the people of New Orleans and surrounding areas. And that was when they had access to all the vehicles and fuel and supplies they needed. If you expect the government to rescue you, you're betting your life on it."

"You make it sound so hopeless."

In many ways, it was. But there was no point to wallowing in despair.

"We should go."

"My fiancé. She's working late tonight. We need to get her. It's on the way."

Cade nodded before taking one last look at the dark expanse of the water. He'd somehow survived a plane crash and drowning and now was stranded halfway across the country from his daughter in Las Vegas and his wife and son in Durango.

He turned away and started walking. Because that was the only way he was going to get back to them.

One step at a time.

14

They headed southeast on Columbus Avenue because it was a straight shot to the financial district and also because it was a wide city street. Cade felt the acute absence of defensive firepower and wanted as much space to react to potential threats as possible. They threaded their way through the maze of vehicles clogging the road. His head on a swivel and senses attuned for danger.

Many cars had been abandoned, but many still had people in them. The doors locked and windows rolled up. Their occupants eyed him and Hudson suspiciously as they passed. Several had already been broken into. Shattered windows and doors left open the evidence of the crimes.

Small groups of people flitted by here and there.

Darker shadows sliding through the surroundings. Some with flashlights swinging back and forth before they disappeared around a corner. A few even said hello as they passed, like this was all just another evening in the city.

They would find out the truth soon enough.

The thin shell of civility and cooperation that was required to make any large gathering of people possible would begin to crack once people realized that the situation had fundamentally changed. When they realized that life as they knew it one minute before the event was gone. And it wasn't coming back for a long time, if ever.

They passed an elongated pyramid-shaped building and entered the tall canyons of the financial district. The height of the surrounding structures swallowed the moonlight.

Cade walked with his fingers clasped around the headlamp so that it emitted just enough light for them to see what was directly ahead. And hopefully not enough to attract unwanted attention.

They had to make a run for it when a group of thugs started after them. But the chase ended minutes later either because they were too fast or because their pursuers had never been intent on anything more than harassment and intimidation.

Whichever it was, it would get more serious at some point. Predators like them and others would stalk the streets searching for easy prey.

They continued on and eventually stopped in front of a brick building with a sign hanging above the glass door.

Furry Friends Day Care

Hudson pushed the button beside the door.

"That's not going to work," Cade reminded him.

"Oh, right." He knocked on the glass and waited. "Amelia is a certified Canine Care Professional."

"You mean like a dog sitter?"

"Well, yeah, only with a certificate. She's studying to become a Vet Tech. Sometimes, I think she's more devoted to animals than me." He rapped on the glass again. "Not really, but kind of."

"I know the feeling." He didn't add that it was the opposite with his dog, Dennis. Sam loved Dennis as much as anyone could love a dog, but Cade loved him like a third child. In her mind, there was a clear distinction between their children and the dog. In his mind, it was less clear.

A young woman appeared at the door and waved at Hudson before letting them in. "Honey, what are you—"

Hudson fell into her arms and started crying.

"Amelia, oh my God. I love you so much. I thought I'd never see you again."

She hugged him tight while Cade secured the door.

"Hudson, what happened? Are you okay?"

He sniffed back the tears and they pulled apart.

She eyeballed the clothes. "What are you wearing?"

"They're his clothes."

She shot Cade a questioning look. "What's going on here?"

Cade and Hudson took a few minutes of rapid-fire back and forth to bring her up to speed. But the look on her face made clear she was having a hard time believing any of it, especially anything about the EMP and what it meant.

It was hard to blame her.

But in the end, Cade didn't care. Whether she believed it or not, it was real and they needed to get moving. He had no desire to be wandering the streets of San Francisco in the early hours of the morning. "Listen, do you have any groceries at home?"

"Uhh, not really," Hudson said. "We do takeout or delivery pretty much every night. There are so many delicious ethnic food places in our neighborhood."

"Nothing in the fridge?"

He shrugged. "A bottle of Sriracha and a few beers."

"What about non-perishables?"

"You mean like canned goods and stuff like that?"

"Yep."

"I don't know. Some crackers. Oooh, half a bag of wasabi peas."

"What about a flashlight, emergency radio, extra batteries, stored water, basic medical supplies? Any of the basics?"

Amelia offered a thin smile. "We have a box of band-aids."

Cade shook his head. These people had the means to be reasonably prepared for emergencies and yet chose to live like every day would work out just like the one before. That was fine, until it wasn't. But by then, it was too late.

"Do you have any cash?"

Cade had a couple of hundred dollars tucked into a secret compartment inside his belt, like he always did when he was traveling, but he couldn't afford to donate a single dollar. Not with the journey ahead.

Hudson dug out his wallet. "I've got forty bucks."

"What about at home?"

They both shook their heads.

Cade ran a hand over his face.

"Hey, it's no problem. I have credit cards and there's an ATM in our building."

"Those won't work anymore. Whatever digital money you have in the bank is probably gone for good."

They didn't like the sound of that.

Cade didn't either. Especially considering all the money he'd just earned was in the same boat. His stomach grumbled and for the first time in a while he realized just how hungry and depleted he was. He dropped his bag and rifled through the contents.

A stainless steel water bottle, an Israeli bandage, a first aid kit, a magnesium fire starter, disposable lighters, cotton balls soaked with Vaseline for tinder, a headlamp, a mini flashlight, spare batteries, a multi-tool, two hundred yards of 550 paracord, the Rand McNally compact road atlas, a compass, sunglasses, sunscreen, compact binoculars, work gloves, a plastic poncho, an emergency bivvy bag, an emergency wind-up radio, duct tape, water purification tablets, an N95 dust mask, black Sharpie markers and tablet of paper, extra socks, extra underwear, no other clothes because they were wearing them.

Most of it in Ziplock baggies and interior pockets to keep it clean and organized.

He found the energy bars and pulled out a bag full of them. A blue Sawyer Mini Water Filter fell out and rolled across the tile floor. Cade grabbed it up and tossed it back into the bag.

"What was that?" Hudson asked.

"It's a portable water filter."

"Why do you carry it around in your bag?"

Cade didn't feel like getting into it. And especially not with two people that, while nicer than many, were completely clueless when it came to being prepared. He decided to keep it short and sweet. "In case I ever need it."

Amelia cast him a dubious look. "Are you one of those survival *preppers* like on TV?"

The way she said preppers told him all he needed to know about her feelings on it.

"If you're asking me if I believe it's a good idea to have a few basic essentials on your person when you're traveling far from home, then yes, I'm a prepper."

She shot a sideward look at Hudson.

"Listen, most of the idiots on TV are purposefully chosen to be entertaining in the most ridiculous way possible. I saw an episode of one of those shows where a self-proclaimed prepper decided to max out his credit cards buying TVs and other junk. He wasn't worried about paying it off because he knew the world was going to end any day. That's stupid and is the exact opposite of the whole point of responsible self reliance. So yeah, I'm a prepper and that means I have a bag of things that often comes in handy on any random day, and especially in an emergency situation."

He opened the Ziplock and tore into an energy bar. "Anybody want one?"

Amelia shook her head like it was fried cockroaches on offer.

"Yes, thank you," Hudson said as he held out a hand. No doubt he was just as hungry after their strenuous swim and subsequent walk to get there.

Cade thought for a minute. He could leave right now. Head out and go his own way. These people weren't his problem. They had their own destinies to deal with. Then again, he needed them as much as they needed him right now. He didn't know anyone in the city and had no place to stay. With fatigue coming on strong, he needed a few hours rest before getting out of the city.

So, for now, he'd help them as best he could and later they'd go their separate ways.

"Is there a grocery store still open at this hour?"

Hudson nodded. "Yeah, there's a little corner market a block from our place."

"Good. We're going there now. You're going to spend that cash on things that will help keep you alive."

Amelia turned to Hudson. "He's scaring me, Hudson. I don't like it."

He wrapped an arm around her and pulled her close. "I don't like it either. But what if he's right?"

The kid was starting to get it. A little.

But he was going to have to get fully up to speed and quick.

15

Another fifteen minutes of walking and they made it to the corner market before closing time. A few lights were on inside and the sound of a portable generator humming somewhere in the back drifted out.

It was a typical corner market in a big city. A small stock of fruits and vegetables. An equally paltry inventory of non-perishables. The liquor and beer selection, on the other hand, took up half the store. Every kind of lottery ticket imaginable was displayed around the register.

"Closing soon," the old guy behind the counter said.

Cade grabbed a basket and went straight for the canned goods. He threw in cans of tuna, baked beans, fruit cocktail, Vienna sausages, green beans, corn, beef stew, a jar of peanut butter, and a number of other items until it was definitely more than forty dollars.

Amelia frowned as he passed. "Is any of that organic?"

Cade almost laughed. He would've if it hadn't been so serious. Sure, he was a big proponent of organic. Eating foods laced with pesticides was one reason so many people were getting cancer these days. But that was a discussion for the normal world.

This was no longer the normal world.

Cancer wouldn't kill you in thirty years if you starved to death in thirty days.

"They're calories that won't spoil," he said as he unloaded the basket on the counter. It wasn't much. A couple of weeks of food if they rationed it. But it was infinitely better than the empty pantry they currently had.

The cashier tallied up the prices by hand on a piece of paper. The bar code scanner and register, of course, didn't work.

The bell hung above the door rang as someone entered.

"Get on the floor! Now!"

Cade turned to find three huge goons standing

by the door, each wielding a pistol. One of which was pointed at his chest. They had the drop on him. One squeeze of the finger and he was a goner.

"Okay, whatever you say," Cade said as he lowered to the floor.

Hudson and Amelia did the same. Hudson did his best to cover her body with his.

One of the others approached the counter. "Don't do anything stupid, old man! I will splatter your brains on the wall!"

"Get out of my store!" the owner yelled back. "Go!"

A shuffling sound from behind the counter and the goon in front fired several rounds.

The sound of a pump-action shotgun being racked and then BOOM!

The guy's chest exploded out his back, spraying the other two in red mist. He collapsed like a rag doll.

The other two fired wildly and the shotgun went off again. The glass store front shattered and shards blew out onto the sidewalk.

The two left jumped out of the missing window.

"He killed Calvin! Shot him dead!"

"We'll be back for you!"

A few wild shots sprayed inside and then they ran away.

Cade lifted his head and took a breath, thankful that they'd been lucky. He turned to check on Hudson and Amelia.

And realized he was wrong.

Hudson knelt over her, pulling her head into his lap.

Her lavender sweater was covered in blood. The red leeching through the fabric as it leaked out of her chest. She gasped over and over like a fish out of water. Aspirated blood bubbled out of her mouth. She coughed and sprayed it on Hudson's chest.

And then she was gone.

"Amelia. Amelia," Hudson said as he held her tight. "Amelia!"

Cade got up, glass crunched underfoot as he stayed low and hurried over to the guy that had taken a shotgun blast.

He was gone.

Cade grabbed up the pistol and saw that it was a Glock 19. An older generation model than the one he had at home, but an effective weapon all the same. He ejected the magazine and found four rounds left including the one in the chamber. He palmed the magazine back in and approached the shattered window, ready to fire.

The street was quiet outside.

He checked the dead man's pockets and found keys, a full magazine, and a roll of money that he'd count later.

He crept around behind the counter. A streak of red along the back wall from where the owner had been hit and then slumped to the floor.

The poor old man sat there, crumpled over, holding his belly as a pool of red grew around him.

Cade dropped down beside him. He pulled the man's hands away. He had an Israeli emergency bandage in his bag. It didn't work miracles, but it was good for keeping pressure on a wound. "Let me see."

As soon as the hands came apart, Cade knew it was no use. The owner had minutes left. Maybe he would've had a chance if an ambulance and EMTs could've rushed to the scene and whisked him away to a nearby ER. But nobody was coming for him.

The doomed man was trying to say something, but choked on blood and couldn't get it out.

Cade couldn't save him, just as Hudson couldn't save his fiancé. So he did the only thing he could, he held a dying man's hand and waited for the end to come.

After the owner was gone, Cade closed his eyelids and said goodbye. He grabbed the shotgun and plucked out the spent shells. An ancient, double barrel break-action model. Probably passed down from generation to generation. Not his first choice for a defensive firearm, but he was thankful to have it. He scanned the vicinity and found a partial box of shells under the counter. He loaded two and dropped the rest into his pocket.

He stood up and saw a bright yellow streak blur through the air and then explode.

Two more came after and a flash of searing heat washed over him.

The two goons from before took off, yelling and swearing.

Cade jumped over the counter and watched in horror as the back of the store was engulfed in flames. They'd thrown in Molotov cocktails and the place was going up fast.

He hurried to Hudson and dragged him to his feet. "We have to get out of here!"

Hudson reached for Amelia, struggling to stay with her.

"We have to go! Now!"

Rougher than he wanted to, he shoved Hudson toward the exit. He tucked the Glock in his waistband and scooped up the basket of groceries on the way out.

Black smoke roiled out of the window and rose into the air as they made it out onto the sidewalk.

Hudson stood there like a zombie. Broken and lifeless. He stared at the bright orange flames as they closed in around the body that had been his fiancé.

It wasn't something anyone should ever have to see.

Cade spun him away and pushed him forward. "We're going to your condo. Lead the way."

Hudson shuffled along, just aware enough to point at the high rise building as they came upon it at the end of the block.

Cade managed to drag him up twenty-nine stories and into the condo. He escorted the poor kid into the bedroom and let him collapse on the bed. He threw a blanket over him and figured he should've done something more, but he had nothing left. He was numb with exhaustion and close to shutting down.

He dropped onto the couch, tucked the pistol down into the cushion within easy reach and kept the shotgun across his chest. Whatever had kept him going this long now deserted him completely. His body was like a battery drained of juice.

There was nothing left.

His last thoughts before nodding off were of his family. Sam had Ethan and Dennis, not to mention Gary next door. How long would it take for her to understand the severity of the situation?

And then there was Lily. She was far from home with her best friend in Las Vegas. Piper was a sweet girl, but she wasn't going to be any help to his daughter. All alone and he was far away.

He had to believe she could make it.

Lily was strong. Stronger than she knew.

But was she strong enough?

16

Lily stood outside the entrance to the Paris Hotel, stunned into silence. They'd seen the destruction from the viewing platform at the top of the tower. But here at ground level was something else entirely. Dim light from the moon above mixed with flickering orange from nearby fires. Burning plastic or oil scented the air, leaving a foul residue in her mouth. Cries of distress and confusion played like a background track to a Hollywood blockbuster where the hero would arrive and save the day.

Only, there were no heroes.

Not any that would be able to fix the multitude of tragedies unfolding along the strip.

She slipped her hand into Piper's. "We have to get back to the hotel."

Piper didn't answer, her eyes wide and soaking up the horror.

"Piper, do you hear me?"

She nodded.

"Okay, let's go."

They started south on Las Vegas Blvd, giving a wide berth to the people they passed. Some wandered aimlessly, clearly stunned with shock. Others huddled together in small groups, speaking in low voices. A figure darted out and sprinted across the street. A few seconds later, three others followed in hot pursuit. They cursed and yelled threats as they pursued their prey.

Lily and Piper came upon the first intersection and a jumble of wrecked cars. A line was crammed together like they had all rear-ended the one in front. Two more were T-boned together where one had hit the other in the side. A dark sedan had the front passenger door open. Moaning sounds and a woman's faint pleas for help came from inside.

"Help me...please...someone... help..."

Piper started toward it and Lily grabbed her wrist. "No, we can't."

Piper's brows pinched together. "What? Why not?"

Lily dropped her head. "We can't try to help

every person that needs it. There are too many people. We'll never get back and it's too dangerous out here."

Piper's expression morphed into one of righteous indignation. "So we just ignore all this and blissfully head back for a good night's sleep? What's wrong with you?"

Lily chewed her lip. She didn't like it either. It wasn't in her nature to look the other way when someone or something needed help. Heck, she was the only one in her family that adamantly refused to smash spiders, moths and other insects in the house. She insisted on taking them outside. Her dad and Ethan went with the bottom-of-the-shoe approach. Her mom was somewhere in between.

But this was different.

She remembered how her dad had warned her about the fragile nature of modern society. About how civility for some people was only skin deep. And that didn't even count the outright criminals. And there was no police presence that she could see. And if there was trouble, the local police would have no way of getting to the scene in any kind of reasonable time frame, much less even know that anything had happened in the first place. Without working mobile networks, most people had no way to report a problem.

No, they had to get back to the hotel as soon as possible.

"I know it sounds horrible, but we have to look out for ourselves right now. Is trying to help someone worth getting into situations where we could become victims ourselves?"

Piper shook her head and marched over to the car.

Lily had no choice but to go along. She wasn't going to abandoned her best friend.

Was she?

What if it came to that?

How far would she go to survive?

She pushed the thought away. She shined her headlamp inside the car and found a middle-aged woman pinned against the steering wheel. The windshield was a shattered web. No airbag that might've lessened the impact.

The woman turned to the light, her eyes glazed and unfocused with pain. "Help me...please..." What had once been a light-colored blouse was now darkly patterned with red. A sickening gash along her hairline streamed blood down her face. A matching splotch of red on the windshield showed how she'd gotten it.

"It's going to be okay," Piper said.

Lily wondered if she believed that or was just saying it to comfort the woman. Either way, it was the right thing to do.

Lily circled around to the driver side door and wrenched it open with a loud screech. She touched the woman's shoulder to get her attention. "What's your name?"

The woman stared blankly for a few seconds and then answered. "Tracy."

"Okay, Tracy. We're going to help you."

She teared up. "Thank you...thank you so much."

"Can you move?"

Tracy shook her head. "My legs are stuck...I can't feel them..."

Lily swept the light lower and saw the problem. The force of the impact had pushed the dash back onto her. A puddle of blood covered the floorboard around her feet. If this woman had any chance of surviving, they had to stop the bleeding.

But that was impossible with the dash and wheel smashed into her body.

Lily found the seat controls and tried to move the

seat back. Not surprisingly, that didn't work. "Do you think you can scoot out if I help?"

"I don't know...maybe."

"Okay, let's try." Lily wrapped her arms around the woman and gently pulled.

The woman shrieked with pain. "Stop! No! Oh God, no!" she yelled and broke down crying.

"Sorry," Lily said, barely keeping it together herself.

She hadn't budged an inch. Pulling at her was only going to cause more pain.

"Piper, help me try to lift the dash."

Piper climbed in through the passenger door and they took hold of the dash on each side of the woman.

"One, two, three," Lily said and they both heaved upward, grunting with exertion.

There was a creak, but no movement.

They blew out a breath and let go.

Lily looked over to Piper and shook her head. There was nothing they could do. She was bleeding heavily and they couldn't get her free.

The woman touched Lily's arm, making her flinch. Her nerves were keyed up and on edge. "I'm so thirsty. Do you have water?"

Lily grabbed her metal canteen out of her backpack and shook it. Empty. She'd meant to refill it after they'd drained it in the casino, but had forgotten. She poked her head out and looked around.

There was a Walgreens on the corner. There was even a light on inside. A security guard stood at the entrance.

Were they actually still open for business?

"Piper, let's go check out that Walgreens. If it's open, we can get some water to bring back."

She nodded.

"Don't leave me…please…don't leave."

Piper sat down in the passenger seat. "Don't worry. I'll stay with you."

Lily chewed her lip. She didn't like the idea of separating.

Piper gestured at the store. "Go ahead. We'll be here."

Lily took off at a jog, knowing that her best friend meant well, but also knowing that it could get them into serious trouble.

17

The security guard standing in front of Walgreen's watched her jog over, his hand on the pistol holstered at his hip. His eyes bounced over to someone shouting on the side street before settling on her again. He held out a hand as Lily got near. "Slow down, kid!"

Lily stopped a few feet away. "Is the store open?"

He scowled, but nodded. "For now, it is. The idiot manager wants to stay open for people that might need supplies."

"Great," Lily said as she started to skirt around. "I need to fill my water bottle."

He dropped an arm to block her. "It's open for paying customers only."

Lily sighed, thinking the manager was probably

more interested in reaping the rewards of panic buying than helping out people in need. "Fine. I'll buy something."

He didn't raise his arm. "Cash only. The registers are down."

"I've got cash," she snapped back, definitely not happy with the way the guard seemed to be enjoying the power play.

He gave her a sarcastic smile, but then raised his arm like a toll gate. "Welcome to Walgreens."

She shot him a look and then hurried inside. There was a long line of customers cued up at a single register. The cashier was a boy around her age and he was not doing well.

"Come on, already!" someone near the back of the line yelled. "We're gonna die of old age in here!"

The boy waved in apology while scribbling furiously on a piece of paper.

Lily found the bathroom sign and headed toward it. She threaded through the aisles, relieved to see them filled with products just like they would be on any normal day. The next question that rose in her mind put a damper on that though.

How much longer would that last?

She got to the bathroom and filled the canteen. She was about to leave but paused.

How much longer would water come out of faucets?

Especially in a city in the middle of the desert. She vaguely recalled her dad saying that it depended on the design of the municipal water system. In places with water towers, gravity could keep the water flowing for a few days. Until the towers ran dry and there was no power to refill them. In places that depended on pumps to distribute water, faucets could go dry in hours.

Which meant she needed to drink all she could while it was easy to get. She gulped down the whole bottle, filled it up again and drained that one too. Sure, she'd have to pee in half an hour, but she'd be hydrated. She filled it up a last time and headed out.

She stopped in the food aisles, scanning the options to decide how best to spend her limited cash. There was more in the Get Home Bag back at the hotel, but this was it for now. A part of her wanted to buy ice cream and cookies. A pretty big part, to be honest. And she would have if this had been a normal night.

But it wasn't normal and so she had to think about it with a different mindset.

What would provide fuel and calories to burn?

She snagged a couple of candy bars because they

had lots of calories and she was craving one anyway. She also grabbed up a handful of beef jerky. The protein would be good. She added a jar of peanut butter because that had loads of protein and calories and the oil was high in fat. A few protein bars and she cued up at the end of the line.

There were fifteen or twenty people in front of her. Most of them looked frustrated, but were doing their best to remain calm. Most, but not all.

A few were making comments loud enough to reach the boy up front. He finished with a customer and waved the next one over. The line inched forward.

"I swear to God if you don't hurry up, I'm going to walk out of here without paying!" The same guy that had been yelling when she came in. He was in the middle of the line.

"Do you hear me, pimple-face? Hurry your shit up!" He spun around a second later and glared at the guy behind him. "Did you just say something? You wanna say it to my face this time?"

The other guy mumbled something and took a step back, clearly not wanting to get into a confrontation.

He didn't get what he wanted.

The complainer set a case of beer on the floor

and, as he rose up, took a swing and connected. Hard. He jumped onto the guy and drove them both to the ground, already landing more punches.

The guy underneath covered up and flailed around trying to escape.

People yelled and screamed. Some trying to stop it. Others egging it on like it was an after school fight and they wanted a good show.

The security guard raced inside with a baton held high. He brought it down on the back of the complainer.

The guy groaned and fell over. And then a revolver was in his hand.

The guard reached for his gun, but had no chance.

Pop! Pop! Pop!

Three shots hit him in the chest. He stood for a second, clutching at the navy blue shirt. And then collapsed.

A few people in line ran for the door, carrying away the things they had been waiting to purchase. As soon as they made it, most everyone else did the same.

Lily edged behind an aisle shelf, eyeing the exit and wondering if the insane guy with the gun would shoot her on the way out.

He stood up and turned to the man he'd attacked. He pointed the gun at his face. "You shoulda kept your mouth shut!"

Pop!

Lily took off, knowing a bullet would find her next.

18

Lily raced back to the car and found Piper inside with her knees gathered up and her face buried between them. She moaned as a spasm shuddered through her.

"Piper?"

She looked up with tears in her eyes. "She's gone."

Lily looked over and saw the truth of it. She went around to the other side and leaned the woman's head back against the seat. She felt for a pulse on the carotid artery in the neck, but there was none. She blew out a breath. "Piper, we have to go."

Piper's head dropped between her knees.

Lily circled around and helped her out of the car.

A pained grimace hung on her best friend's face. "Why is this happening?"

Lily didn't know if she meant why North Korea or Iran or whoever had attacked them or if she was asking why bad things happened. It didn't matter either way because she didn't have the answer.

"I don't know, but we need to go. And Piper," she said as she held her by the shoulders and leveled a serious look, "we can't stop for anyone else. The longer we're out here in the dark, the more chance there is of running into trouble."

"Okay," Piper said and the two started south toward the hotel. "How far do you think it is?"

"A couple of miles. We should be there in forty to forty-five minutes."

"I'm supposed to walk for a couple of miles in these?"

Lily bit back a harsh reply. Getting into an argument wasn't going to help. "We can break off the heels. It wouldn't turn them into comfortable sneakers, but it would be an improvement."

Piper crossed her arms over her chest and pointedly didn't answer.

They continued south a while and Lily breathed a sigh of relief when she recognized the silhouette of the hotel a few blocks away. Piper was slowing down in those ridiculous shoes and if she got any slower, something was going to have to be said.

A whistle pierced the air.

"Hey, ladies! What are you doing out at this hour?"

Lily turned to see a group of five gangster-looking guys walking toward them, right down the middle of the cross street. Pants hanging low, faces hidden in the depths of oversized hoodies. A few of them carrying half empty bottles of booze. The one in front with a thick gold chain hanging from his neck. Their flashlights converged on the girls like a spotlight.

"Piper, run." She pushed her in the opposite direction.

Piper took two steps and landed wrong. A shoe twisted under her and a heel snapped off. She hit the pavement knees first and cried out in pain.

Lily dragged her up and they ran as best as they could, which wasn't great with Piper limping along with bloodied knees and one shoe missing a heel while the other was still intact.

"Where you going, baby?"

Gruff laughter and then the pounding sounds of pursuit.

Lily spotted the entrance to New York New York

on the left. The doors were closed and the interior dark. The same with the Beerhaus next door.

They kept going. Bits of glass crunched underfoot as they weaved through a knot of wrecked vehicles and emerged into a sculpture garden. She glanced over her shoulder and saw the gangsters catching up.

There was no way they were going to outrun them. They had to lose them and fast.

"Squid, go around that way!"

Lily scanned left and right as they kept going. The store fronts were dark and doors shut. If they stopped to try one and it turned out to be locked, that would be it.

She glanced right and saw one of them coming up an alley. They were closing in. She saw an escalator going up to the second floor of a parking garage. It wasn't a great option.

It was the only option.

Lily steered Piper toward it. "Go up!" she yelled as they arrived at the stationary steps.

Piper's shoes clacked against the metal steps as they raced up. They made it to the top as the leader with the gold chain arrived at the bottom.

He smiled, and not in a friendly way.

Lily's heart hammered against her ribs, her

breath coming in heaving gasps. They ran into the shadowed interior of a packed parking garage. They crouched low trying to stay beneath the roofline of cars as they cut through the maze of vehicles. An idea came to her and she tried a door handle.

Locked.

The leader arrived at the top of the escalator. "We're coming for you, hot mamas! And we're gonna have some fun when we catch you!" The others laughed with malignant glee.

"We have to find a car to hide in," Lily whispered as they continued on. She tried a few more cars with no luck. Then the handle on an old gray Honda Accord clicked. "Here!" she hissed. She carefully opened the back door, terrified that it would squeak and broadcast their position.

It was quiet enough.

A foul odor hit her in the face and she wrinkled her nose in disgust. The back seat was piled high with all kinds of junk. Newspapers, magazines, books, wadded up paper napkins, bathing towels, stuffed animals with their insides spilling out, clothes, shoes, blankets, crunched up beer cans, a styrofoam container with the lid open. A pizza box with the moldy remains of a slice inside.

Someone was living in this car. A hoarder.

Lily guided Piper inside and followed her in. They had to dig their way through the mountain of debris. She closed the door and fumbled around in the dark for the lock. She tapped the button a few times but nothing happened.

Of course!

She cursed at herself for the stupidity. "Push the lock down," she whispered to Piper as she took care of her side. "Check the front too." They both ensured all four doors were locked and then sank into the shadows behind the front seats. The pile of junk filling the rear seat completely covered the back window.

"You trying to hide from us?"

She recognized the voice now. The one with the gold chain. The ring leader of their perverted posse.

A beam of light flashed over the window, but thankfully didn't stop.

An explosive shatter and Lily realized they must've smashed out a nearby car window.

"We know you're in here! Come out now and I promise we won't hurt you!"

More laughter and loud banging on cars. They were whooping and celebrating like their team had just won the Super Bowl.

"Spread out and check under the cars! They're in here somewhere!"

Piper was curled into a ball, crying hard but barely making a sound. She understood the danger.

Lily found her hand in the dark and it was shaking uncontrollably. She squeezed, trying to offer some reassurance that she didn't feel herself.

A shadow passed by the side door glass and then was gone.

Minutes passed as they listened to the ongoing search. The terror of being found and knowing they were trapped. The stench in the car so thick it was hard to breathe.

"They must've got away, man!"

"Bullshit! They ain't wizards! They can't just up and disappear!" The leader again. "They're hiding in a car! That's it! Search the cars!"

19

Donny bit off another bite of burger and tossed the remainder onto the dash. He chewed a few times and then spat it out the window. He liked Big Macs as much as anyone, but this one had been tasteless from the beginning. It wasn't McDonald's fault.

It was the casino's.

They'd stolen his money.

Not just what he'd won fair and square, but what he'd come in with too.

Lady Luck had done him wrong. That was no surprise. He'd always had to make his own luck and make his own way. Sure, this time left him lower than usual because he'd never been so close to having it all.

When that steel ball had landed on black, he'd

completely lost his mind. It was like the clouds opened and a ray of sunshine came through. For the first time in as long as he could remember, something went his way.

It was a turning point.

It was the start of the future he always knew was out there waiting for him.

And then just as fast, it was gone.

Snatched away by some kind of freak power outage.

Talk about bad luck.

Talk about Lady Luck taking a huge dump on his head.

"You gonna finish that?" Zeke said, his eyes darting to the discarded Big Mac.

"Go for it," Donny said. He wasn't hungry. Nothing was going to taste like anything ever again until he made it right with the bastards that stole his money.

Zeke wolfed it down and wiped his mouth on his sleeve like a two-year-old.

Donny flung a stack of napkins at him. They flew apart like a flock of birds and perched all over him with white wings spread. "Use a napkin for once in your damned life! I swear to God I feel like your mother sometimes!"

Zeke kept his mouth shut and used one of the napkins, now that it didn't matter and the special sauce was streaked on his sleeve.

Donny blew out an exasperated sigh. Not for the first time, he wondered why he chose to hang around with such a loser. And also not for the first time, he remembered that he didn't have any other friends. And that they had a long history together. From escaping an abusive foster home in their early teens to growing up on the streets together.

They'd always had each other's back.

There had even been a time or two when Zeke pulled both of their butts out of the fire.

Donny smacked the steering wheel and then silently apologized to the Mino.

"What's up?"

"I'm pissed about what happened!"

"Yeah, that was messed up."

"You got any crank left?" Donny could already feel the emptiness growing inside. The need that started out small but didn't stop there. He was pretty sure he had a secret stash back home, but that didn't count for much right now. There was a tiny rock in a baggie hidden up under the dash. Barely enough for both of them to get fried.

"Nope," Zeke said as he gathered up the napkins and then tucked them into the glove compartment.

Donny took a long pull off his soda and shook the cup to feel how empty it was. About right. "You got that rum?"

Zeke grinned and reached under his seat. He pulled out a brand new bottle of Captain Morgan Spiced Rum. Zeke was too much of a coward to pull off a proper heist, a fact that Donny brought up after each and every one of his successful convenience store jobs, but he did have a special talent at boosting merchandise.

He never left a store empty-handed. Well, the hands might've been empty, but the pockets and waistband weren't.

After Zeke paid for burgers at McDonald's, he'd only had a few bucks left. All the cash that was left for both of them. They'd gone to the liquor store and Donny bought a pack of smokes while Zeke wandered the aisles. Even with an employee tailing him the whole time, he'd somehow managed to lift that bottle of rum.

Zeke spun the lid off and passed it over. "Go ahead. You can say it."

Donny snatched it away and filled his cup. Half rum, half Coke was about right. Too much Coke and you lost the burn of the islands. Too little rum and what was the point?

"You're good," Donny said as he swirled it around with the straw. "I've said it before and I'll say it again."

Zeke poured and mixed his own drink. "Say what again?"

"Shut up." Donny sparked up a smoke and drew in a hot, deep breath. The end of the cigarette glowed orange with the air crackling through it. He tossed the pack over because there was plenty for now and also because technically it was Zeke's cash that had bought it in the first place.

He opened his mouth and let the smoke seep out. He blinked away a tendril that curled up into his eye. Another long drag and he waited for the nicotine to kick in. It was no substitute for speed, but it was still good.

They drank and smoked in silence for a few minutes while Donny stared at the casino across the street. He knew what he wanted to do. The problem was that it was crazy. Knocking off a few convenience stores didn't make him an expert.

Casinos were another level. They were famous for having tight security. A tweaker he used to run with had found that out the hard way. The idiot snatched up a bunch of chips and ran for it. Might've just gotten a beat down for his troubles.

But then he pulled a knife and the security muscle took that real personal.

The moron ended up in ICU for months. When he finally got out, he couldn't talk right. They'd permanently scrambled his brain. He vanished a while after that. Maybe he took off or maybe that casino finished the job.

It didn't matter either way. They'd made an example of him. A broadcast that made the rounds loud and clear. Trying to rip off a casino was a high risk game. And failure was a lot worse than spending time in the county lock up.

Donny had never seriously considered knocking off a casino, even before that happened. The risk versus reward just didn't make sense. Sure, it did in Hollywood movies, but not in real life.

But it was different this time.

They'd stolen his money and he couldn't let that go. Besides needing it to pay off Jax, it was a matter of respect. If he let this pass, word would get around that he was a chump. Life on the streets was hard enough without everybody thinking you were an easy target.

No, he had one and only one choice.

"Donny, what are we going to do? Jax is going to kill you for sure."

Donny blew out a cloud of smoke at his friend. He turned back toward the casino. "He'll get his money."

"How?"

Donny flicked the butt of his cigarette out the window. "We're going to go over there and take what's mine."

20

Donny hauled a duffle bag out from behind the seats and settled it in his lap. He slid the zipper open and fished around inside. His fingers found the cool metal of a barrel. He pulled out a pistol and held it out.

Zeke shook his head. "Are you crazy?"

"Stop being such a pansy. It's not an electric eel. Take it!"

Zeke took the gun, holding it like a wild animal that might turn on him any second.

Donny retrieved another pistol and set it on the dash. Next came the ammo. He checked and loaded each in turn while Zeke stared in silence.

Next, he dug out a flashlight and a couple of rubber Elvis masks. They were late Elvis. The overweight, drugged up days. A swoop of black hair on top, huge sideburns and gold-framed glasses that were part of the mold. Poorly painted and oddly warped from the latex being too thin. The King of Rock and Roll, resurrected by some factory in China.

He'd used them on the previous jobs and it had worked out great. Whatever footage the cameras got would show some Elvis robbing the store. And Las Vegas was a town chock full of Elvis Presleys. There were hundreds of potential suspects cruising around on any given weekend.

He handed one over.

Zeke let it fall in his lap. "No way. I'm not going."

Donny knew this was coming. "Listen, man. There's nothing to worry about. I mean, look around. Nobody's got power. And you heard those explosions. Sounded like bombs going off." He flicked a finger up and down the street. "And those fires are still going. You think the cops are gonna ride to the rescue?"

"I'm not worried about the cops! With them, you have a pretty good chance of getting arrested. Casinos are different, man. They play for keeps. You know what they did to One Shoe."

The tweaker. Stupid name, but that was all anyone ever called him.

"One Shoe was an idiot. You think I'm an idiot?" The question had an edge to it. A warning.

"No, of course not. I'm just saying it's too dangerous. We'll probably get shot!"

"No, we won't. And me not paying off Jax is a guaranteed death sentence. You said it yourself. He'll kill me. And what do you think he'll do to you?"

Neither of them knew for sure, but Jax had a reputation for getting carried away. It wasn't a stretch to think that they would both end up in an unmarked grave somewhere in the endless desert.

"Dammit, Donny! You know I'm not cut out for this."

Yeah, he knew it. But he needed backup and the pathetic moron in the passenger seat was all he had.

"I know. On any normal day, I'd never ask. But this ain't a normal day, man. This is the first day of the rest of our lives." He puffed up a little, thinking that last part came out pretty smooth.

"Yeah, this is the last day of our lives."

So much for smooth.

"Look, it was chaos in there when we left. It's been a while, but you know they haven't gotten it all sorted out yet. We have to strike now while we have the chance."

Donny ferreted out the baggie and pipe. The last

of the meth would get them cranked up and ready for action. He let Zeke have the first hit which wasn't something he usually did.

They passed the pipe back and forth until it was gone.

Donny breathed through the electric splinters, his fingers tapping the side of the gun like piano keys. All of a sudden, the rush hit and it was time. "Let's go!"

He wondered if he'd have to threaten Zeke into action, but the speed was working its magic, giving his buddy an extra dose of courage that would last as long as the high did.

They slipped on the masks and got out.

Zeke came around with the pistol in hand.

Donny grabbed his arm. "Keep that pointed at anything but me, okay?"

"I know that!" The gun was vibrating in his trembling hand.

Not the best back up, but whatever. Too late to worry about it.

"Come on." Donny grabbed him by the shoulder and they jogged across the wide street. "If anyone points a gun at me, you shoot them. Okay?"

Zeke didn't answer.

Donny spun him around so they were face to

face. "You hear me? You watch my back and we'll get out safe and sound. Ready?"

Zeke straightened his mask so he could see better out the eyeholes. He nodded half-heartedly.

Donny grinned, but the mask hid it. He tried the door and found it locked. Not a problem. He aimed at the glass and fired.

They climbed through the metal doorframe and Donny clicked on the flashlight.

The interior was still dark. People hurried here and there using their phones for light, paying no attention to anything not immediately in front of them. It looked like a tornado had blown through. There was crap everywhere. Overturned tables and chairs. Bright glints of glass reflecting off the floor. Clothes that had been left behind in the rush to get anywhere else.

Donny noticed a particularly nice brown leather motorcycle jacket draped over a chair and snagged it as they passed. He stuffed it into the duffle bag hanging on his shoulder and continued on toward the cashier's cage.

They turned a corner and nearly ran over some idiot. The guy's hands shot up and he backed away after Donny pointed the pistol at his face. He wasn't going to kill him. Not for no reason. He wasn't some sicko that got his rocks off by making people bleed.

Not like Jax.

They made it back to the cashier's cage without incident and Donny was starting to have a good feeling like this was all going to go according to plan.

And then he noticed all the cashiers were gone.

He cursed under his breath as the plan started to crumble.

They got to the cage and quickly tried all the cashier windows. All locked. And it wasn't like he was going to shoot through bars that thick.

He twisted the flashlight around, playing the light up and down on the inside of the window.

There!

The lock that held it shut.

"This is gonna be loud." He aimed the muzzle at it, looked away and fired. It took another shot, but it worked.

He whooped with joy. The lock had been blown clean off. A hard shove and the window scraped up. He was considering making Zeke crawl through but decided against it. A few too many Big Macs had rounded out Zeke's belly. The last thing they needed was him getting stuck in there.

"Keep an eye out!" Donny shouted as he jumped

up and wriggled feet-first through the narrow opening. It was tight, but he managed to squeeze through.

He turned to the nearest register and tried to pull the drawer open. Locked. He smashed it with the butt of the pistol but got nothing out of it but a tiny dent.

"Dammit!" he yelled in frustration and then hammered it over and over, hoping the stupid thing would open up eventually.

It didn't.

It bent and crumpled and keys flew off like popcorn on a skillet. But the drawer didn't come out.

He yanked at it a few times, but it showed no signs of getting looser.

The plan was definitely falling apart now.

Donny spun around, searching for anything of value. A woman's purse was tucked into a cabinet under the counter. He found a wallet inside with ten bucks in it.

He slung it against the bars, positively fuming with fury. He hadn't come back to score a few measly dollars! He wanted his money!

"Drop the weapon!" a voice shouted from behind.

He turned with the pistol in hand.

The gun pointed at him fired.

A bright spark as the bullet ricocheted off the cage.

Another gunshot and the security guard jerked. One more and he crumpled to the floor.

Donny turned to see Zeke with his pistol raised, smoke leaking out of the end of the barrel.

More voices shouted in the distance. Security guards and they were coming quick.

Donny wriggled out and jumped to the floor. He grabbed Zeke by the elbow and dragged him along. "Time to go!"

Shots fired as they ran out the front entrance, but none found their mark.

They sprinted across the street and Zeke stupidly headed straight for the Mino.

"This way!" Donny shouted. If the guards came after them, he didn't want the Mino getting shot to pieces. They ran around to the back of the Panda Express and fell against the side of the building.

Panting for breath, listening for sounds of pursuit.

There were none.

The guards weren't coming after them.

They slowly edged to the corner and peeked around. The street was quiet and nothing hinted at what had just gone down.

Donny chewed on the inside of his already ruined cheek. He tasted blood and hacked out a loogie.

What was he gonna do now?

Jax wasn't going to accept another excuse. And while Jax was open to payment in various forms, Donny had nothing to offer. The Mino was all he had that was worth anything and Jax would laugh in his face if he offered it as partial payment.

Besides, the Mino was too good for that uppity bastard. There were abandoned cars left in the street. Some of them real nice, but they'd tried them a while ago. None started for some reason.

What else was worth serious money?

The kind that could clear his debt and then some.

Whatever it was, he had to figure it out soon.

Because he was running out of time.

21

Samantha steered the portable generator through the side door of the garage and wheeled it out to the back patio. "Ethan, I need those cords!"

"Coming!" Her gangly son came out with thick bundles of orange cords lassoed over his shoulder. He dropped them next to the genny and started untangling the mess. "You think Mr. Hensley is right?"

"I don't know. It does sound like what your father told us about. And I don't know what else would make sense."

She didn't want to scare him, but she also didn't want to downplay a situation that could very well be a catastrophe in the making. If Gary was right about it being an EMP, then they were all in trouble.

A dagger of worry stabbed her in the chest.

Lily was in Las Vegas with her best friend. She was eighteen and had long ago established a solid foundation of trust between them. She'd promised to stay out of trouble and be back Sunday night. Sam had every confidence that she would hold to her word.

Even Cade had finally agreed to the trip and he wasn't an easy sell. She'd had to talk him into it. But now, she wondered if she'd made the biggest mistake of her life by doing so.

Lily was smart and capable, but she still was just eighteen. And if this turned out to be anything like Cade had described…

She couldn't let herself think about it.

All the things that could go wrong.

A part of her wanted to pack up this instant and drive the five hundred plus miles to get to her. A big part.

But was that overreacting?

Was that letting her anxiety take over?

And then she remembered Cade's truck wasn't working anyway so it didn't matter.

If this was some kind of EMP event, then her old Volvo should still work. That meant the girls could get home. For now, she had to trust that they would do exactly that.

"Mom?"

Sam blinked awake and saw Ethan staring at her.

"You okay?"

"Yeah, I'm fine. Just worried." She found the right cords and got them plugged in. The genny fired up on the first pull—she made a mental note to thank Cade for his diligent care–and they had the refrigerator, a few lights and a power strip hooked up a few minutes later.

They settled on PB&Hs with chips for dinner so they could keep the fridge closed. The H stood for honey, and it was just as good as jelly for anyone that wasn't a sandwich purist. She didn't want to run the genny overnight and the fridge would stay cold enough so long as they kept the doors shut.

Which was easier said than done.

Ethan opened it once on accident looking for something. She grabbed the handle a few times and nearly opened it herself. And that was just during dinner. It was so automatic. Wonder what's in the fridge. Open the fridge and look.

So she put a strip of blue tape across the handles as a reminder.

The kids used to have an annoying habit of

opening the fridge and staring inside like it was a puzzle they couldn't figure out. They'd stand there for minutes at a time, pulling something out, putting it back in, thinking about another option.

It used to drive her and Cade crazy. She'd gone full mom-mode one time and took a picture of the contents, printed it out and taped the paper to the door. It had actually worked for a few days. They stared at the paper instead of standing hypnotized with the doors open.

But a few days of eating changed the inventory and she didn't update the picture. So it was back to fridge hypnosis.

A few summers ago, it had seriously turned into a thing in their house. Parents versus kids. Constant haranguing and resulting resentment. Cade had finally landed on the idea that changed it for good.

They got charged a quarter every time they got caught doing it. Ethan ended up losing his entire allowance for a month before he changed his ways. Lily wasn't as thick-headed as her brother. It took her less than two dollars to get on board.

"It's your move," Ethan mumbled through a mouth full of sandwich.

"Right. Sorry," she said as she glanced at the Otrio board. Otrio was like Tic-Tac-Toe, only for grown ups. Once the colored rings and pegs started filling up the board, it got really hard to keep track of all the possible moves. It rarely ended in a tie, which was something that Tic-Tac-Toe hadn't delivered since elementary school.

Ethan tossed a chip to Dennis who was lying on his bed in the corner of the dining room. He snapped it out of the air like a frog hunting a fly.

"I saw that," she said. "No feeding from the table. You know the rules." She picked up a large green ring and held it over an empty groove in the board.

"Sure you want to do that?"

"Not now," she replied and scanned the board again. He'd long ago been crowned the de facto Otrio champion of the house. She spotted where he was about to win and blocked it, clicking the ring into the groove with a triumphant smirk. "Your move."

He nonchalantly placed a red peg in another spot and won the game. He shrugged. "I had two ways to win."

They reset the board and played another round while they finished dinner. She didn't win. They cleaned up, ran through the evening routine, and decided to go to bed early.

Sam shut the genny down and made sure the

house was locked up before retiring to the master bedroom. The master bedroom that had felt conspicuously lonely for the last two months.

She folded the sexy black nightie and tucked it into a dresser drawer. It and the champagne would have to wait. She found the chocolate in her purse and tore open the wrapper. A few ravenous bites later and it was gone.

Chocolate never lasted long.

A while later, she was in bed with the covers pulled up and a Kindle in hand. Thank God it still worked. Slipping into a story was the only way to shut off her mind sometimes.

Night was when all the worries came out of the woodwork. And there were far more than usual with Cade and Lily so far from home. And worse, she didn't know if they were safe.

Sam tapped the screen on and picked up where she'd left off the night before. It took six chapters before she finally got drowsy enough to fall asleep.

She set the Kindle on the bedside table and closed her eyes.

She could worry more in the morning.

22

Something jarred her awake!

She blinked a few times, expecting to see the soft blue glow of the nightlight in the hall.

But it was dark.

Was she still asleep?

The muffled sound of Dennis barking like crazy echoed down the hall from Ethan's room.

She was definitely awake and angry now that she realized why. That hyperactive dog was going to wake up the whole neighborhood. She grabbed her headlamp off the side table and swung out of bed. Dennis was going to get it for scaring her half to death!

Her heart hammered in her chest as she hurried to Ethan's room to see what was the matter. She threw the door open, ready to scold Dennis for this middle of the night freakout. She'd barely opened it when Dennis pushed it open with his muzzle and burst out.

He raced downstairs, still barking like crazy.

And that was when she heard a knock at the front door. The knock drove Dennis into another frenzy of growling and barking.

Who would be at the door at this hour?

She considered going back to the bedroom closet for the Glock 19 they kept in a safe. But then thought better of it. She was overreacting. She didn't want to open the door wielding a gun. It was probably the other neighbor Brenda Finch over to complain about something. That woman had been a pain in the ass from the minute they'd met. She was so self-centered and self-righteous that anything and everything had to be someone else's fault. A perpetual fake smile plastered on her face communicated equal parts disdain and derision.

And she got spiritual joy in finding something to complain about.

The side irrigation was spraying on her sidewalk making it dangerous for her to walk on her own property. Never mind that the sidewalk was technically owned by the city.

Ethan's bike got left out one night and she didn't want to attract a criminal element with easy pickings.

They'd have to get rid of the azaleas because she was horribly allergic. How did they expect her to breathe in her home with those toxic weeds right next door?

She found poop in her yard again and knew it belonged to Dennis. To be fair, it had once or twice.

Sam headed downstairs, already angry about whatever that crazy woman was going to say this time. She stopped at the door, petting Dennis to calm him down and also to thank him for doing his job. She flicked on the porch light, but it stayed dark. She jiggled it a couple of times before remembering it didn't work.

She peeked through the blinds covering the side window and saw an agitated-looking Gary Hensley standing outside. A flashlight bouncing against his leg. She unlocked and opened the door, holding onto Dennis to keep him under control.

"Gary, what time is it?"

He glanced at his watch. "Almost midnight. Sorry to wake you."

Dennis' tail wagged like crazy and his whole body whipped back and forth with enthusiasm.

Sam let him go before he yanked her arm off.

Gary scratched his muzzle. "It's good you have him. He's better than any home security alarm."

"Gary, what's going on?"

Gary looked up with a frown wrinkling his face. "I've got some terrible news. You remember Ms. Conway over on Borrego Drive? Hers is the ugly purple house at the end of the block."

Everyone in the neighborhood was familiar with that eyesore and the woman who proudly claimed it.

"Yes, of course."

His mouth flattened into a tight line. "She's dead."

She was older than Gary and so definitely in her golden years. It was sad to say, but more than a few folks in the neighborhood were going to be thrilled that her house would be sold and repainted.

"I'm sorry to hear that. Did she have some kind of condition?"

He shook his head. "Not that I know of and that's not what happened even if she did. She was murdered. Bludgeoned to death in her own kitchen."

"What? When?"

"Not too long ago. The neighbors heard a commotion and went to check on her. They were too late."

"How did you find out?"

"Couldn't sleep and was working on my scanner. Damn EMP fried it. But I've got buckets of spare parts so I might be able to fix it. Anyway, my two-way radio squawked. It was local PD reporting in about the incident."

"Did they catch whoever did it?"

"Not that I've heard." He rubbed behind Dennis' ears, another one of his favorite spots, as evidenced by his eyelids closing. "Just thought you should know. Be a good idea to make sure all the windows and doors are locked."

"I checked before going to bed."

"Do you know how to operate a firearm?"

"Do you know my husband?"

Gary flashed a smile and nodded. "Might be a good idea to keep one handy until the killer or killers are collared."

"You think there's more than one?"

"Don't know but if you prepare for the worst, then you'll never be surprised."

Sam peered over his shoulder at the dark houses across the street. First this power outage that was likely something far worse. And now there was one or more murderers on the loose?

What was happening to the neighborhood?

To the world?

She gave him a quick hug. "Thanks for letting me know."

He pulled back uncomfortably, but smiled. He was too old school for hugging and hugging another man's wife in the middle of the night was way outside of his comfort zone. He gave Dennis a last scratch. "You keep an eye on things, okay, buddy?"

Dennis barked and circled around behind her. Cade always said he was the smartest dog in the world. It was times like now that she almost believed it.

"I'm right next door if you need anything. And I don't sleep for shit so I'll hear if anyone comes sneaking around our street."

"Thanks, Gary."

"Night," he said as he tipped his head and then marched away.

It was only then that she noticed a large caliber revolver tucked into the back of his pants.

Was this their new world?

People had to walk around carrying guns to feel safe?

Or worse, to actually be safe?

23

A car door slammed shut nearby, sending a jolt of terror up Lily's spine. The fine hairs on her arms stood on end like lightning was about to strike.

One of the gangsters searching for them was getting closer. If he stopped at the car and looked inside, he'd see them. And they'd already smashed out plenty of windows so the locked doors weren't going to save them.

An idea came to her.

A repugnant one.

But it might help.

"Piper," she whispered. "Cover up with all this junk."

Her friend grimaced but started pulling what

amounted to trash on top of her. Lily helped and she was buried in no time.

She started scooping garbage on top of herself. A takeout container with a mound of moldy yuck inside. A metal fork too. She grabbed the fork. Another scoop revealed a crusty wad of dirty underwear. That was too much. She tossed it to the side and kept scooping.

The voice outside grew louder as she frantically pulled an avalanche of refuse onto herself and then settled beneath it. The stench had been bad before, now it was eye-watering. She sipped tiny breaths to keep from gagging.

She waited in silence, balled up as small as possible and covered in filth. She prayed Piper didn't make any noises that might give them away.

The front driver side door handle jiggled.

Another spike of fear jolted through her. She gritted her teeth together to keep quiet. Piper was somehow managing to do the same.

"This one's locked."

A light swept over the backseat, filtering down through the heap to reveal a red hairbrush inches from Lily's nose. A clump of long black hair was matted into the bristles. She wanted to push it away, but dared not move.

"Yo, take a look at this! One of them packrat types."

More light flooded in through the window. "That's messed up. People like that are for real crazy. I seen a show on it. They called hoarders. They buy stuff all the time and don't even use it. And they can't throw nothing away. Doesn't matter what it is."

"Is that a filthy pair of underwear?"

"This ain't nothing. People on the show had whole houses full of crap. Piled to the ceiling."

"Hey, check that out!"

"What?"

"That's leather pants with the tag still on. Looks about my lady's size too."

"Are you seriously gonna score something from that trash heap?"

"Why not? She'll never know."

"Whatever. Do it and let's get back to searching. They didn't get away. I know that."

Lily flinched when the window exploded, showering them in bits of glass.

Piper screamed.

"They're in here! They're in the car!"

More glass shattered as the side window on Piper's side was knocked out. The one with the gold chain got the door open and reached in for Piper as Lily popped up out of the heap.

Piper thrashed away and he had a hard time getting a hold of her with all the junk flying around.

He latched onto an elbow and yanked her up.

Lily grabbed Piper's other arm and tried to pull her away. But he was too strong. It was tug of war and she wasn't going to win.

Another jerk and Piper's arm slipped from her grasp.

Screaming for her life, Piper lashed out and caught the guy with a hard kick to the nuts. It must've landed perfectly because he doubled over with a groan.

The window on Lily's side exploded in and a hand reached in to open the door.

"No!" She slammed the fork down just as it found the handle.

A howl of fury and pain as the arm jerked away.

A face appeared at the window, the leader again. "You're gonna pay for that, bitch! I'm gonna hurt you good!"

The others were around the car now, clamoring to get the girls out, shouting vile promises of what would happen next.

A gunshot split the air.

Lily thought for half a second that she or Piper had been shot. But no, it didn't look like it.

The gangsters surrounding the car turned away and returned fire. Bullets thunked into the car's body panels. "Go!" the leader yelled as he skirted around toward the hood. A few more shots and then they were gone.

"Hello?" a voice said.

Piper curled into a ball on top of the pile, trembling violently as the tears poured out.

"Anyone in there? It's okay. You're safe now." The voice closer now.

Lily didn't know what to do. Who was coming? Were they really safe?

A bright light and a figure appeared in the window. A flashlight blinded her for a second before it shifted to the side. A police officer with his gun drawn. Hard eyes that softened in an instant. He scanned the interior and then holstered the pistol. "Are you hurt?"

"I don't know," Lily said as he helped her out. She stood and a dizzy spell made her wobble.

The officer held her steady while giving her a quick once-over. "Come on." He guided her over to a curb and helped her take a seat.

He went back and helped Piper out. In her case, he helped by carrying her over like she weighed next to nothing. He eased her down to the curb and Piper fell into Lily's offered arm. Lily noticed the broad chest and hard muscles bulging through the khaki uniform. The shiny star pinned to the long-sleeve shirt finally made it click in her mind.

The attack was over.

"My name is Officer Rivera. I work for Las Vegas PD." He touched the star. "You can trust me. What are your names?"

"Lily and Piper," Lily said indicating each of them in turn.

"Are either of you injured?"

Lily pointed at Piper's skinned knees.

"Anything that would require a trip to the ER?"

"No, I don't think so."

"Good. Listen, normally I'd drive you down to the station and help you out there. But my cruiser is dead so that's not an option."

Piper pulled her head out of Lily's shoulder in a panic. "You're not leaving us, are you?"

He dug a handkerchief out of his pocket and handed it to her. "No. Of course not. I can't take you to the station, but we can't stay here either. Those degenerates might come back. Where are you staying?"

That assumed they weren't locals.

What gave it away?

Plenty, probably.

"Mandalay Bay," Lily said. "We were walking back when those creeps came after us."

"That's almost a mile south. Too far in the dark with things like they are."

"Where are we going then? Piper asked.

"The T-Mobile Arena is next door. I was doing off-duty security there when the power cut out. The place is empty now, but I still have the keys. You can sleep in one of the luxury suites. There's couches and chairs. No blankets but plenty of clothes scattered around."

The worry that Lily felt must've translated to her face because he smiled reassuringly.

"I know it sounds crazy. I hear myself saying it. But it's not safe out here in the dark. Come morning, I'll escort you to Mandalay before hiking back to the station. Lord knows I want to get there before the heat picks up."

He helped them both to their feet.

"I know it's not great, but this is the best I can

offer considering the circumstances. Ready to move?"

"Yeah," Lily replied. "And thank you… for saving us."

"Glad I heard the commotion when I did."

24

The inside of the T-Mobile Arena pushed Lily's already fragile nerves to the breaking point. Pitch black with cavernous ceilings high overhead. The sound of their footsteps swallowed by the massive space. Jackets, coats, scarves, shirts and other unidentified clothes scattered everywhere like the bodies wearing them vanished into thin air. The sour smell of spilled beer confirmation of what had created at least some of the sticky patches on the floor.

Officer Rivera led the way, his duty flashlight bouncing a bright beam back and forth as they went. He scooped up a jacket but it didn't pass the sniff test. He dropped it and kept going. "Grab anything that looks like it will keep you warm."

They passed by shuttered concession stores, the floor was particularly sticky there.

Lily spotted a random shoe when she had an idea and snagged it. This one a sneaker that should fit Piper. She kept an eye out for another on the opposite foot and found it on the stairs they took to the second level.

Piper didn't notice. She was trudging along in a daze. A three inch heel on one side and not the other giving her a pronounced stagger. Her eyes locked on Officer Rivera and nothing else.

"One more set of stairs to the luxury suites," he said over his shoulder.

By the time they got to the suite, Lily had a pile of clothes and Piper's new sneakers in her arms.

Officer Rivera unlocked the suite and ushered them inside. "This is the Executive suite."

Lily sucked in a breath.

She was imagining something like a little hotel room without the beds. It was that, just way bigger and nicer. She'd been impressed with the double room at the Mandalay, but this was real luxury.

A sleek onyx black countertop ran along the right wall. A line of silver pots on top that looked like a squadron of UFOs about to take off. Stainless steel appliances and cabinets underneath. A tall narrow table floating nearby covered with the remains of the feast that had been served that night. The left half of the room a swanky assemblage of white couches and chairs surrounding a low glass table that looked like it had somehow melted up out of the floor. Half-empty glasses and plates of food on top. The far wall made of partitioned glass with metal tracks in the floor so the suite could be opened or closed to the action outside.

Officer Rivera set his light on the low table, pointing it up at the ceiling to bounce the glow around the space. He guided Piper over to one of the couches and covered her with a couple of jackets. He started clearing away the leftovers, moving them over to the buffet table. "The food's still good if you're hungry."

Lily dumped her things on the opposite couch and then joined Piper. She flinched away when Lily touched her.

"It's me," Lily whispered.

Piper nodded and leaned into a hug.

"We're going to be okay. Officer Rivera is here."

He gathered up another round of dishes. "Call me Manny. I know it's the last thing on your minds right now, but you should try to eat something. It'll make you feel better."

Lily remembered Piper's knees and wanted to clean those up first. "In a few minutes." She retrieved the small first aid kit from her backpack and pulled out some anti-bacterial ointment along with a few of the larger band-aids. She scrounged up some clean napkins and bottles of water from around the room and then knelt in front of her friend.

Piper stared at her, not crying anymore, but not well either.

"Piper, I'm going to clean these cuts, okay?"

She nodded.

Lily got to work cleaning and dressing the wounds. She was finishing up when she noticed Manny watching.

"Do you always carry a first-aid kit in your bag?"

"Yeah, it's kind of a rule with my dad."

"Smart guy."

Lily tucked the kit into her bag. It used to annoy her that he insisted she have what he called an Everyday Carry bag. Okay, maybe annoy was an understatement. It drove her crazy and made her the butt of more than a few jokes at school. It had been an ongoing point of friction between them until they'd finally compromised their way to an agreement.

First and foremost, he'd had to agree to stop

calling it an Everyday Carry bag. It was her backpack. He'd also had to agree to her removing some things she considered totally unnecessary or too heavy to lug around every single day. A magnesium fire starter. She had a couple of disposable lighters instead. A two-thousand calorie food bar that was as heavy as a brick. She had energy bars instead. An extra pair of socks and underwear. Too weird and they always fell out at the worst possible times.

Though they would've been nice to have now.

The other thing that helped settle it between them was that she found herself actually using different things from time to time. Tweezers to remove splinters. The mini sewing kit when her old backpack blew a strap. The paracord when Dennis' leash got lost on a day hike.

"Where are you from?" he asked.

"Durango," Lily said as she spread clothes out over the couch. She'd get this one ready for Piper and then make the other for herself. "We were here to celebrate her getting married. You know, the whole wild weekend before tying the knot thing. So much for that."

"Sorry it didn't work out. I've never seen anything like what happened today. But don't you worry. We'll have everything up and running before long."

Lily forced a smile. It was good to hear his optimism, she just didn't share it. She made up a plate of leftovers and forced herself and Piper to finish it. Then, she helped Piper settle down and covered her with a patchwork blanket. She covered the other couch with random clothes and laid down.

Piper was already out.

Manny was sitting in one of the chairs, nibbling from a plate in his lap while reading a magazine.

"Can we leave the flashlight on?"

"Sure thing. It's LED. It'll last for days."

"Thanks," Lily said as she pulled a suit coat up to her chin.

25

Lily jerked awake. The sound of an exploding car window echoing in her mind.

Had it been only in her mind?

Piper was sleeping on a couch across from her.

Why was she on a couch?

Lily bolted upright, disoriented and falling toward panic.

The flashlight on the table bounced light up to the ceiling and around the room. And then she remembered.

Being attacked. Being saved.

Officer Rivera.

Manny.

He wasn't in the chair.

Her head swiveled around as she searched the

room. He wasn't in the room either. She checked her watch.

7:14AM

They'd slept through the night. The sun was up and they could get back to the hotel, pack up, and get on the road.

Where was Manny?

The only thing the suite was missing was a bathroom. Maybe he'd gone to take care of business and didn't want to wake them.

Maybe.

Still, she didn't like it.

She swung her feet to the floor and stretched out an aching back. A yawn crawled out of her mouth and a whiff of bad breath followed. She gently woke Piper and was happy to see her looking better after a decent night's sleep.

"Good morning."

Piper scrubbed at her puffy eyes. "You sure?"

Lily rolled her eyes. Piper was famous for hating on mornings. "The sun is up. We need to go. I want to get on the road by nine."

Piper looked around in confusion. "Where's Officer... what's his name?"

"Rivera. I don't know. I woke up a few minutes ago and he wasn't here. Maybe on an urgent bathroom break."

She nodded. "Reminds me I have to pee."

"Me too."

They got up and around and picked through the parts of the buffet that didn't require refrigeration. There wasn't much left. Olives, crackers, some cheese that was still good, chips and salsa.

Piper popped the last olive into her mouth. "Breakfast of champions. At least it's free."

"I wonder what's taking Manny so long."

"Manny?"

"Officer Rivera."

"Oh. Yeah. Let's go find the bathrooms and yell at him for scaring us."

Lily presented the mismatched sneakers she'd scavenged. "Put these on first."

Piper looked at them and then at her like she was crazy.

Lily waited, tapping her foot to emphasize that this was taking too long.

"You want me to wear someone else's mismatched shoes?"

"This isn't a discussion. Your heels are ruined and they're terrible for walking anyway."

Piper glanced at her shoes by the couch. They were indeed ruined. "Fine." She put the sneakers on and then made a face. The *are you happy now?* one.

"How's the fit?"

She stepped back and forth a few times. "Not bad. I look ridiculous, if you care about that."

"Ready?"

"Sure."

Lily slung the backpack over her shoulder and grabbed the flashlight.

She pulled the door open and morning light flooded in. She clicked it off, but kept it handy because it was two foot long and heavy and that meant swinging it at somebody would do some damage.

The chaos of the night before was even more evident in the morning light. How many people did the arena hold? And how hard would it be to get that many people out in a calm and orderly fashion?

Clearly, pretty hard.

They found the women's bathroom and both relieved themselves. They both guzzled a ton of water and Lily topped off her canteen and a water bottle before leaving. The men's bathroom was a little ways down and they stopped at the entrance.

"Hello? Manny?" Lily called.

No answer.

"Officer Rivera, are you in there?" Piper said as she tip-toed closer and peeked around the corner. "Oh my God."

Lily went around and saw the reason for the reaction.

Lying on the concrete floor by the sinks was the man that had saved their life. He was dead. Throat cut with a puddle of blood surrounding his upper body.

His gun was missing. Whoever killed him had taken it. Must've snuck up and slit his throat.

Lily dragged Piper out.

She was already starting to hyperventilate and not far from melting down completely.

Lily was barely keeping it together herself, but both of them falling to pieces wasn't an option. She held her finger to her lips.

"Quiet", she mouthed.

Piper's eyes went wide. She understood.

What if whoever killed Manny was still there?

"Let's go," Lily whispered.

They tip-toed through the wide halls, down the stairs, cringing every time a misstep made a noise.

Lily shoved the door open and they fled outside into the bright light. They kept running. All the way to the giant black pyramid that was the Luxor Hotel.

There was the Mandalay!

Piper pulled Lily to a stop. She leaned over, holding her knees, breathing hard. "Let me… catch my breath."

The Mandalay was less than a block away!

But Lily resisted the urge to drag her forward. It was light out and there were even a few random people hurrying around on whatever business a morning like this had for them.

Lily stowed the big flashlight in her backpack and waited for Piper to recover. Piper wasn't exactly the athletic type. She loved her curves and claimed that too much exercise would ruin her figure. Hating every form of exercise might've had something to do with it too.

It was fine. They could afford to take a minute to rest.

They'd finally made it back.

Tires squealed down the street.

An old primer-colored car jumped the median and roared up the wrong side of the street. It raced around abandoned cars and nearly lost control, before straightening out.

It was headed right at them.

26

Donny was having the best damn dream of his entire life. He knew it was a dream and it didn't matter. He was laying on a reclined chair by an enormous pool, those fancy ones where the edge just disappears. A couple of topless honies were splashing around in the water, giggling and carrying on.

The pool was accompanied by a mansion. *His* mansion. Though he didn't recognize it, and he couldn't remember ever having lived in anything remotely like it.

One of the girls popped up out of the pool like a seal. Water streaked down her boobs and Donny knew he'd paid for them. And they were worth every cent.

She wiggled over to him because that was what

walking did to her. It made her wiggle in the best way. She leaned over him, showing off a new angle that reaffirmed the thousands spent. "Donny."

"What?"

"Donny."

"What?"

She moved and the sun blasted him in the face.

"Donny, wake up."

Donny's eyelids peeled apart and it was horribly bright.

"Donny, wake up, man."

Donny turned to see Zeke in a sorry state. "You look terrible."

"You got the smokes?" Zeke asked.

"What?"

"The smokes, man! You had them last."

Donny blinked a few more times, still adjusting to the idea of being awake, angry that the dream was already fading. He let out a yawn and looked around. They were in the Mino parked out front of McDonald's. He spotted the pack of cigarettes on the dash. He tapped one out before tossing it over. He lit it up and drew in a long breath.

The warm smoke seeped into his lungs. The first hint that maybe today was worth living. He drew in another to be sure. The dream had been so real. It was already fading fast but he remembered enough.

The girls.

The money.

The power.

It was like a vision of his future. A vision that could become real if he just reached out and claimed it. Everything he'd ever done had gotten him to this point. And before passing out last night, he'd finally for the first time in his life understood why.

Why was he dead broke sleeping in the Mino with this junkie loser for his one and only friend?

And why was a man like Jackson Cook running things? Why did he have all the girls, all the money, and all the power?

Because he could.

That was why.

The revelation had come through so clear and obvious. Donny had always thought small and so lived a small-time life. Jax thought big and so it was no surprise that he was big-time.

Donny took another drag as he considered his next move. He still hadn't landed on the next big score.

"I killed a man, Donny," Zeke whispered.

Not this again. Zeke had carried on half the night wringing his hands like a little school girl. Donny was sick to death of hearing about it. "It was him or me, man. You did what you had to do."

"I guess so."

"There's no guessing. It's his fault if you get down to it."

"Yeah, I wouldn't have shot him otherwise."

"See? Exactly. Now, shut up and let me think."

They finished their smokes in silence and fired up a couple more because Donny wasn't done working through the problem.

He was racking his brain for the solution when he looked up and there it was.

Two girls standing out front of the Luxor hotel. One bent over, probably barfing through a hangover. Both young and both good looking.

One of Jax's many business ventures was selling girls to upmarket clients. Sex slaves. He'd get them hooked on H, break them in until they were nice and compliant, and then move the merchandise for a handsome profit. Runaways mostly because they didn't raise any flags when they went missing.

Donny fired up the Mino and slammed his foot on the gas.

With all the insanity going on, with cars and

phones not working, it would be a lot easier for folks to simply disappear.

And unlike sticking up convenience stores and casinos, the risk would be next to nothing. No guns blazing at them as they dashed out the door.

Donny's head smacked the roof as the Mino jumped over the median. He jerked the steering wheel over, barely missing an abandoned car. He steered around a few more and nearly lost control when the Mino fishtailed sideways. He somehow managed to get it under control and hammered the accelerator.

The girls were staring at him like deer in headlights.

He wrenched the wheel over and slammed on the brakes. The back of the Mino whipped around and nearly took the girls out.

"You drive!" Donny yelled as he jumped out with a pistol in hand.

He grabbed the curvy girl around the waist and lifted her.

The other one jumped at him but he smashed the butt of the gun into the side of her head and she fell to her knees.

The curvy girl came to life, but he slapped her hard and she calmed down. He shoved her over into the bed of the Mino and went back for the troublemaker. She was still stunned, so it wasn't too hard to dump her into the back too.

Some guy in the parking lot at the Luxor shouted. "Hey! Stop!"

Donny fired in the general direction and vaulted into the back. "Go!"

The Mino peeled out as Donny dropped on top of both girls. One was still not all there. She'd be trouble when she woke up. But he could handle trouble.

He turned to the curvy one and grabbed her by the hair. "Keep your mouth shut and stay down or I'll kill you both!"

She whimpered in response.

He saw the terror in her eyes. She'd do as she was told.

Wind whistled overhead as the Mino picked up speed.

Donny could've shouted for joy. He'd never imagined it could be so easy. And that was exactly the problem.

He'd never dared to dream.

Well, that was history. The future was a whole different thing. He had a lot of big ideas and this was just the start.

27

Twenty minutes later, the Mino pulled into a driveway in a mostly empty neighborhood near the intersection of Balzar Ave and N. Martin Luther King Blvd. If there was a rougher area in the city, Donny didn't know about it.

This particular neighborhood, Wayward Pinecrest, hadn't always been so run down. Years ago, it had been filled with working class folk doing the best they could to make a life for themselves. Then the housing boom swept through the city like a tsunami, upending everything and everyone. Developers came in buying up empty lots and buying out folks that had never seen so much money flashed in their faces.

The old houses disappeared and cookie-cutter, mini McMansions sprouted up. And then it all went bust. The for sale houses stayed that way and the occupied ones slowly emptied out through foreclosures and evictions. The cheaply built new houses had been abandoned and crumbling for years. Now and then, the city would come in and bulldoze one to the ground when it was deemed too unsafe to ignore.

It was a tragedy for most people.

But not for Donny and Zeke.

For them, it was rent free living.

Zeke jumped out, raised the garage door and pulled the Mino in. He had it slammed shut a few seconds later, which was a good thing because the dark haired girl had been giving Donny trouble.

Donny backhanded her across the face. "Shut up! No one's coming for you!" She wanted to claw his eyes out, he could tell. But she couldn't because he'd taken the opportunity while she was zoned out to zip tie her ankles and wrists. He'd done the same to the curvy girl and she hadn't even resisted. Not after he grabbed her by the throat, anyway.

He and Zeke marched them into the living room and shoved them down onto a grubby old couch. They'd scored it on the side of the road and hauled it back in the Mino. It wasn't no bed, but it was way more comfy than sleeping on the floor.

The dark haired one stared at him like he was the one who should be worried.

Donny knelt in front of her and squeezed her face hard enough to know it hurt.

She didn't let on that it did.

"I like your spirit. Jax is going to like it too. He enjoys breaking the strong-willed ones."

She spat in his face and tried to bite him.

He jerked away just in time and then walloped her with a closed fist this time.

She fell back onto the couch, stunned and moaning.

"We got a wild one here, Zeke." Donny ripped up some cloth and cinched it around the girl's head to keep her quiet. He did the same to the curvy one to cover his bases.

A can of beer cracked open and Donny turned to see Zeke chugging a PBR. "That's the idea, man! Let's celebrate!" He grabbed one for himself and emptied half the can before taking a breath. He swiped at his chin, grinning from ear to ear. "We've got Sugar and Spice and everything nice!"

"What?"

Donny pointed at the curvy one. "That's Sugar and that's Spice."

"How much you think Jax will pay us for them?"

"Pay *us*? Don't you mean *me*? This was my idea, after all."

Zeke's expression hardened.

Donny pinched his cheek. "I'm kidding, man. Of course, us! Don't sweat the details. This is the start of something big. And you're in on the ground floor. You're going to be swimming in more money than you seen in your entire life!"

"That's only if Jax doesn't kill us both."

Donny smacked his shoulder. "Good point. And that's where you come in."

Zeke was already shaking his head.

And Donny was already nodding his. "You have to go to talk to him. Let him know I haven't been ducking him. Tell him about the merchandise. He's a businessman. He'll know profit when he sees it."

"What about our end?"

"He pays half a grand for skank runaways." Donny gestured at what they had to offer. "Sugar and Spice will get twice that each. At least."

Zeke's eyes sparkled. "Two grand? Really?"

"Well, there is the matter of the debt and he's probably tacked on more interest."

Donny thought of the baggie of speed he had hidden in the bathroom. "Tell him we want some more crank too. Enough to have a proper celebration. Maybe we'll even give Sugar and Spice a taste to get them in the mood."

Zeke nodded enthusiastically. They were both feeling the emptiness building inside. The terrible gnawing hunger that had to be fed before it turned ugly.

"That should still leave us plenty in our pockets." Donny finished the beer and tossed it at Spice's head.

She ducked to the side and glared at him.

"See? Spice."

Zeke laughed so hard he blew beer bubbles out his nose.

Donny grabbed another can and dropped into the ratty old recliner they'd scavenged. "I'll stay with these two while you set up the deal. The keys are on the counter."

"You want me to go now? I need something to eat and a few hours of sleep."

Donny leapt out of the chair and swiped the keys up. He peeled open Zeke's fingers and slapped the keys into his palm. "Yes, now. And don't come back until it's done."

Zeke nodded and turned to leave.

Donny slid into the recliner and cracked open another beer.

The door to the garage opened.

"Zeke!"

"What?"

"Take care of the Mino."

"Yeah, okay." The door slammed shut.

Spice looked around the room, her eyes landing on the sliding door to the backyard.

Donny pointed his gun at her. "You think you're faster than a bullet? I don't. But you're welcome to find out."

28

Cade jerked awake with someone standing over him. Not fully aware yet, he grabbed the shotgun and brought it up at his assailant.

Hudson threw his hands up and backed away. "Don't shoot! It's me, Hudson!"

Cade blinked through the cobwebs and realized who he was. He lowered the weapon and set it on the couch. "Right, sorry. Was having a bad dream. Still in it there for a second." He glanced at his watch and then out the floor to ceiling window.

The sunrise on the eastern horizon cast a warm orange glow across the sky. It was beautiful. The promise of a new day. The kind of scenery that inspired artists and gave people hope. Unfortunately, the situation down on the ground didn't reflect that feeling.

Cade stood and stretched, working feeling into his aching muscles. "Bathroom?"

Hudson pointed down the hall. "Second door on the right."

Cade relieved himself and returned to find Hudson poking through the groceries they'd picked up the previous night. He went to the sink and tried the faucet.

Water came out, but it was a quarter of the regular flow.

How much longer would even that last?

He filled up a glass and drained it and then another. He planned on covering a lot of miles today and every day that followed. As many as it took to get to his daughter in Las Vegas.

He looked in the fridge and found a couple of styrofoam containers. They were still cool to the touch. Spaghetti with meat sauce in one and garlic rolls in the other. "Hungry?"

Hudson shrugged. His bloodshot eyes narrowed to a slit.

"Did you get any sleep?"

"Some."

Cade split up the leftovers and slid a plate and a fork across the island counter. "Eat. No sense letting it go bad."

Hudson picked at it while Cade wolfed his down.

He got the Rand McNally atlas from his bag and flipped to the section for California.

"What are you doing?"

Cade didn't look up. "Figuring out how to get to Las Vegas."

"Las Vegas? You live there?"

"No, Durango, Colorado is home but my daughter is in Las Vegas for the weekend."

"On her own?"

"She's eighteen and with a friend. Believe me, I wasn't happy about it."

Especially now. If he'd stood his ground, she wouldn't be there now. It would've been all too easy to let that chew him up so he forced it out of his mind. The important thing was to get to her as soon as possible. A vehicle would've been ideal but the working ones were going to be in short supply.

And they were also going to attract a lot of unwanted attention. And that meant trouble.

The obvious alternative was walking, but that would take forever. Too long. He'd noticed a couple of nice looking road bikes in the bedroom next to the bathroom. He needed one of them. Just had to figure out a good way to ask first.

He used the miles scale at the bottom of the map to measure out the distance to Las Vegas following major interstates. Through Fresno and Bakersfield and then looping east to Vegas. Roughly six hundred miles. On a bike, he could maybe do fifty miles a day. So that was twelve days.

Anything could happen in twelve days. It was far too long.

And that was if everything went smoothly, which it wouldn't. Major highways were going to be dangerous places to be pretty soon. That was because they were obvious routes for people to take. And so anyone that wanted to prey on others would be drawn to them like lions prowling a watering hole.

For the same reason, any government response would also focus on interstates in order to control the flow of refugees.

Cade wanted to stick to smaller roads whenever possible and definitely avoid cities. The good news was that the map showed all kinds of smaller roads that could be used to circle around major population centers. He'd eventually have to cut through Death Valley National Park, which wasn't reassuring. Then again, it was all desert down there.

He wished it wouldn't take so long. That he could snap his fingers and be there. But wishing without doing never changed anything.

Cade finished the spaghetti and got ready to go while Hudson returned to his room. The shotgun went into his bag because any law enforcement they came across weren't going to react well to having it slung over his shoulder. He tucked the Glock into his waistband and smoothed his shirt over it.

He walked back to Hudson's room to ask about the bike and to say goodbye. "Hey Hudson, I noticed those two bikes in your spare room. I was wondering…" He got to the doorway and did a double take. "What are you doing?"

"Packing."

"Why?"

"I want to go with you."

"What?"

The kid was nice and Cade definitely felt for him after losing his fiancé. But him tagging along? Not a good idea.

Hudson folded an orange velvet sport coat into a carry-on bag. "With Amelia gone, there's nothing here for me now. And if it's as bad as you say, I should leave too."

"I'm sorry, but I can't do that."

"You're going to Durango, right?"

"Yeah, after I find my daughter in Vegas."

"I grew up in Albuquerque. My family is there. That's not far from Durango."

Cade shook his head. "I wish the best for you, I do. It's just—"

"You want one of my bikes, don't you?"

Cade's jaw dropped. Was he being black-mailed by this uppity punk?

"Take me with you or no bike." He closed the carry-on bag and zipped it shut.

Cade bit down to keep from cursing. He could just take the damn bike. Beat the kid up if he tried to stop him. That didn't sit right with him though. He was prepared to do whatever it took to get back to his family, but he didn't have a heart of stone.

So that left taking him along, for now.

"Okay. Give me a bike and I'll make sure we both get out of the city."

"All the way to Durango is the deal."

"Nope. No deal." He turned, ready to walk away, or at least bluff that he would.

"Fine! Out of SF and Oakland and then we'll part

ways." He held out a hand and Cade shook it. "Ready when you are."

Cade glanced at the carry-on bag and rolled his eyes. "No, you're not."

29

They rode down the street with backpacks and bags hanging off the sides of both bikes. It had been an exercise in frustration, but Cade had finally succeeded in getting the kid packed. Hudson wasn't happy about relinquishing his bike to Cade, but his smaller frame made more sense for Amelia's bike.

They pulled to a stop in front of the corner mart at the end of the block. Shattered glass covered the sidewalk in front. The interior was a blackened husk. Dark smoke seeped out the missing front windows and swirled away on the breeze.

Hudson leaned his bike against a car and approached the store with a bouquet of purple and white irises in hand. He'd brought them from home and insisted they stop on the way out. He knelt and gently placed them on the sidewalk. He stood and whispered something.

Cade scanned up and down the street, anxious to get moving but knowing the kid needed to say goodbye.

Hudson returned to his bike with tears in his eyes and they pedaled away.

Cade followed him through the city streets as the kid knew the way to get on the Bay Bridge. As they rode, he shifted through the gears and tested the brakes to get a feel for how the bike handled. He didn't know much about road bikes, but this was obviously a nice one. Carbon fiber frame and thin racing tires. Couldn't have weighed more than fifteen pounds on its own.

So why did an expensive bike like this have such a ridiculously uncomfortable miniature seat?

The towel he'd duct-taped around it was a little awkward, but he preferred that to chapped buttcheeks.

The city streets were mostly empty. Of people, anyway. Cars were another matter. They were everywhere. Packed together in long lines that rose and fell over the hills. Dark columns of thick smoke rose in the distance.

They glided through an intersection, staying close to the curb where the path was less obstructed.

Hudson suddenly swerved up onto the sidewalk and Cade saw why.

A homeless man was sprawled out off the curb, half in the street. He might've been sleeping were it not for the caked blood surrounding his head.

Disasters hit the most vulnerable first. For people that were already hanging on by a thread, it didn't take much to finish the job.

Hudson zipped through some trashcans and then jumped the curb back onto the street.

Cade had to pedal hard to keep up. They rode through a labyrinth of streets and made a hard left turn onto the exit ramp of the bridge. The Bay Bridge stretched seven miles from San Francisco to Oakland. The westbound lanes were stacked on top of the eastbound ones for half of that length.

So, they were technically riding the wrong way against traffic, but it didn't matter and Cade preferred the open air to the enclosed lanes below.

The space between cars opened up as they made it onto the main span of the bridge itself. Despite snarls of wrecked vehicles here and there, there was usually enough space for them to get by without slowing down much.

The deep green expanse of the bay opened on both sides. The briny scent of the ocean filled his lungs. Cool morning air chilled the sweat beading on his forehead.

They rode by hundreds of abandoned cars and quite a few with people still in them. Some sleeping, some staring as they sped by. Yerba Buena Island drew nearer. It was a small island that connected the two halves of the bridge. Hudson had mentioned that it had a Coast Guard station, radio towers and some other buildings.

Hudson's pace slowed so Cade pulled up alongside to see what was up.

A little ways down, a guy was standing in front of a motor coach, waving his arms and yelling to them.

"What do we do?" Hudson asked.

"Let me handle it," Cade said as he took the lead, eyes scanning for danger. He slowed to a stop fifty feet away and sat up, one hand on the bike and one on his thigh, fingers under the shirt flap and inches away from the Glock.

"Hey!" the guy yelled again as he waved. "Thank God you're finally here!" A rainbow-colored Hawaiian shirt pulled tight over an impressive beer belly. Board shorts and brown flip-flops completed the look. One hand held a glass with a purple umbrella sticking out the top.

He wasn't trouble.

He was clueless.

Cade walked his bike forward, his right hand free in case he turned out to be wrong.

"Hey there!" Mr. Hawaii said with an over-the-top warmth that suggested he was tipsy.

"Hi," Cade said.

"You guys with Triple A?"

Cade stood there not knowing whether to laugh or cry. He shook his head. "No, sorry. I'm afraid not."

"We're on bikes. Do we look like Triple A?" Hudson added, unhelpfully.

Mr. Hawaii looked them over. "Well, I figured you had battery jumpers and stuff in those bags."

Cade didn't like where that was going. "Nope, nothing like that, sorry."

"Well, do you know when help is coming?"

"Can't help you there either."

Mr. Hawaii frowned, like it was somehow all their fault. "How am I supposed to get my family out of here with a dead battery and the road like this?"

The conversation was going nowhere and this idiot was rubbing Cade the wrong way. But he had a family and he was worried about them. Being an idiot didn't mean he was a bad person. "Listen, you should get your family off the bridge. Take what you can carry and get to a safe place. I don't think any of these vehicles are leaving anytime soon."

He hooked a thumb up at the shiny blue motor coach. "You want me to leave Margaritaville behind?"

Cade noticed the side of the bus. An airbrushed scene of a beach and palm trees and a crystal blue ocean. Margaritaville in red cursive letters above that. He didn't want Mr. Hawaii to do anything. He was just offering advice, for whatever it was worth.

"That baby is my retirement. Besides, we have everything we need in there."

"Glad to hear it," Cade said as he steered the bike to the side. "We have to get going."

"Want a margarita for the road?"

Cade swung a leg over his seat. "No. Thanks though. Good luck to you." He pushed off and pedaled away with Hudson following behind. Unfortunately, Mr. Hawaii and his family were likely going to be among those that didn't survive.

They continued on to Yerba Buena Island and Cade saw something he didn't like. The road disappeared into a tunnel carved through the island. It was fairly short. Enough light made it through from the other side that it didn't go pitch black.

But that didn't mean it was safe.

He slowed to a stop and saw a trail off the side of the road that appeared to go over a hill to the other side.

"Why are we stopping?" Hudson asked.

"I don't want to go through the tunnel. It's a perfect spot for an ambush."

Hudson made a face like he was crazy.

Maybe he was being paranoid. Then again, maybe he wasn't. And if they went in there and it turned out he wasn't, it would be too late for a do over.

He pointed at the trail. "We'll take that over."

30

They hoisted the bikes on their shoulders and climbed over the guardrails into a dense thicket of trees. Branches caught on the wheels and handlebars as they picked their way through. The dirt trail led up to a service road that appeared to skirt around the side so they took it.

As they rounded the curve, voices carried on the wind. A lot of voices, but where they were coming from wasn't obvious.

Cade leapt off and carried his bike into the trees that lined the road. He crept deeper into the shadows, senses taut and tuned for potential threats.

Through a thick canopy of green, they saw the source of the noise at the bottom of the hill. A complex of buildings was situated on the waterfront.

A U shape of plain, two-story structures next to a compact assortment of other buildings. A large green lawn enclosed in the U. A parking lot wrapped around it all. A half-dozen ships were anchored at an attached dock. A longer dock extended out into the water with a white Coast Guard cutter anchored at the end.

"I think that's the Coast Guard station," Hudson whispered.

"Yeah," Cade replied. That was obvious. What wasn't obvious was what was happening on the lawn. Cade dug into his bag and fished out a pair of binoculars.

The zoomed view brought it into focus.

A hundred or more soldiers wearing green camo fatigues and carrying M4 rifles. They were hurrying this way and that as platoon leaders barked commands. Out of the chaos, ordered ranks formed up until the last soldier jumped into line.

A door opened in an adjacent building and their commander marched out. He stopped at the front of the formation and began relaying some instructions.

A deep thumping grew louder and Cade spotted a Blackhawk helicopter racing toward the station. It steered to a hover above the empty basketball court and slowly set down. As soon as the skids touched down, the door slid open and two men emerged. One turned to yell back into the chopper. Yellow block letters were printed on the back of his dark navy jacket.

FEMA

The commander met them at the side of the makeshift landing pad and the three got into an animated conversation. The guy in the FEMA jacket pointed up at the bridge and then off toward each end. Apparently, the commander wasn't getting the message because the FEMA official screamed in his face, over and above what was needed to be heard. He snatched a briefcase from the guy that had arrived with him. He pulled out a paper and waved it in front of the commander's face.

The commander calmly took the paper and read through it.

The FEMA official went off again, jabbing his finger at the bridge.

Finally, the commander nodded and the three hurried over to the assembled troops. The commander relayed something and the ranks broke apart. A line of soldiers ran through an archway and started climbing into the back of a transport truck.

"We have to go. Now!" Cade grabbed his bike and headed back toward the road. Branches snapped as he bulled his way through. He jumped onto the seat and took off.

Hudson wasn't far behind and soon caught up. "What's wrong?"

"They're going to shut down the bridge! We have to get through before that happens!" He hammered the pedals around the curve and steered up the on ramp. They merged into the main lanes and picked up speed.

Cade had a death grip on the handlebars while his legs pumped the pedals around and around. The bridge ended a couple of miles away. Visions of military trucks blocking the lanes and cutting them off from escape drove him.

Was it possible that he could fail so soon?

He never expected it to be easy, but this would be a crushing blow.

His thighs burned and his legs ballooned with blood. He blinked through the sweat streaming into his eyes.

It was the longest two miles of his life and yet it was over in minutes.

The end of the bridge came into view.

Along with a convoy of drab green military vehicles. Not from the Coast Guard station, but obviously part of a coordinated action.

Cade pedaled harder, faster.

Stationary cars blurred by.

One pothole or piece of debris would turn him and the bike into a mangled mess.

The bridge ramped down and the city of Oakland sprawled out before them.

The convoy was headed toward them in the opposite lanes. A Humvee peeled off and jumped over the median to intercept them.

Cade's heart dropped. And then he spotted a bike path running alongside the road. He steered over and plunged down a gravel embankment. The bike skidded over and he nearly wiped out. He bounced onto the bike path and the tires chirped as they gained traction and straightened out.

He glanced over his shoulder and saw that Hudson made it too. They sped downhill, leaving the Bay Bridge and the impending blockade behind.

They raced through an industrial area populated with nondescript warehouses and permanently parked delivery trucks.

Cade took a few random turns in case they were being pursued and slowly the scenery changed. Big box retail stores lined the street on both sides. A

Target, Home Depot, Michaels, Panera Bread. A number of hotels.

A few blocks down, a couple of people ran across the street carrying something.

Cade slowed their pace to see what was happening and also because his lungs were about to burst.

They continued on and a figure sprinted across the intersection ahead. This one carrying something too.

They slowed to a stop a little ways off and saw what was happening.

It was a mob scene.

31

A crowd was gathered in front of a Best Buy store. The glass doors had been knocked out and people were shoving their way inside. Just as many people were shoving their way outside, arms filled with stolen goods.

"I didn't know Best Buy still existed," Hudson said.

"That's the first thing that popped into your head?"

"I mean, I thought they went bankrupt years ago. Who goes to a store to buy anything these days?"

"I don't think they're buying."

Two big guys broke out of the perimeter of the mass carrying an enormous flat-screen TV. They both had Forty-niners jerseys on.

"Those two must really like their football," Hudson said.

The joke landed flat, but the fact that he'd even made it was a good sign.

The looting didn't surprise Cade, but he didn't find it funny either. It was a sign of what was coming. The fraying and eventual failure of law and order. The heavy-handed response of a federal government fighting to retain control. The coming crackdown on personal liberties to better control the masses. The splintering of civilization into isolated fiefdoms ruled by ruthless tyrants.

Maybe it wouldn't devolve to that point.

Maybe.

"Wait, they aren't going to be able to watch that TV anyway, are they?"

Cade shook his head.

Other looters streamed out of the store carrying computers, gaming consoles, and more. One lady that looked like an average everyday housewife was dollying out a washing machine.

"Let's go," Cade said. "We don't want to be around when things go south."

Hudson nodded and they got back into gear.

They made sure to swing over to the opposite side of the road in case any of the looters decided expensive road bikes had more appeal than whatever was left in Best Buy.

Sure enough, they were riding through the next intersection when gunshots and screaming echoed down the street. They paused to check it out.

More gunshots and the crowd was spilling into the street, everyone running away at top speed.

"Let's go," Cade said as he started off again.

Hudson didn't move.

"Hudson! We're moving!"

He snapped out of it and caught up a few seconds later. "It's just so crazy. I never would've believed anything like this could happen in our country."

Cade was about to tell him that it was going to get worse, but decided against it. He'd see for himself soon enough.

They continued on a ways, staying in the bike lane which was remarkably free of obstructions. Abandoned cars littered the street. Some missing windows and surrounded by shattered glass. They made sure to ride around those. The last thing they needed was to blow a tube. Hudson had a repair kit and extra tubes, but they would be needed for the long road ahead.

Multi-story apartment buildings rose on both

sides. A group of skaters loitered on the next street corner. One was flipping his board doing a series of tricks while the others watched with cigarettes and bottles of beer in hand. One of the ones watching noticed Cade and Hudson approaching and brought it to the attention of the rest of the group. They turned as one and shouted out colorful threats.

Cade didn't want any trouble and was hoping they didn't either.

The group walked into the street to intercept them, some acting belligerent while others were laughing and clowning around.

Cade pulled the pistol out of his waistband and held it out to the side in clear view. They glided to a stop a good distance from the skaters now blocking their path in the middle of the street.

"We're just passing through. We don't want any trouble."

The one in front wore a sleeveless denim jacket with a green spray-painted pot leaf on the chest. Tattoos sleeved both arms and more scrawled out of a ratty t-shirt across his neck. His head was shaved on the sides with a tall mohawk sticking up in the middle. Hair didn't do that easily. For someone who obviously wanted the world to believe he didn't give a crap, he definitely cared about his hair. If Cade was reading them right, they were the kind that wanted easy prey. They weren't hardened killers looking to take another life.

"This is our street. If you didn't want trouble, you shouldn't have come this way."

None of them were armed that Cade could see. That didn't mean they weren't though. And seven against two wasn't good odds.

"Sorry, we don't know the rules. We're not from around here."

"What do you have in them bags?" Mohawk asked.

"Laundry. Just riding home from the laundromat and took a wrong turn."

It was weak. He knew it as soon as it came out.

"Thought you weren't from around here?"

"Well, not this neighborhood."

"Give us the bags and you can go," Mohawk said as he started forward. The rest of his crew fanned out behind him.

Cade lifted the Glock and aimed it at him. "I'm afraid we can't do that."

Mohawk started to reach behind his back, maybe for a gun tucked into his pants.

"Don't do it! You don't want to die today!"

He laughed derisively, but stopped coming

forward and stopped reaching for whatever it was. He looked left and right at his crew. "Be smart. Drop the bags and get the hell out of here. Think you can take us all down?"

"Hudson, back away," Cade whispered. In a louder voice, he answered. "No. But I can definitely kill you from here. Two to the chest before moving onto your friends."

The grin on Mohawk's face faltered.

Good.

He didn't have a death wish. Cade's read on the group was more or less right.

Cade backed away with the muzzle zero'd on Mohawk's center mass. If he did have to fire, he'd take him out and dive behind a car for cover. With any luck, they'd scatter after seeing one of their own killed.

Mohawk watched as they retreated. His face twisted with a mixture of fury and uncertainty. One of his crew launched a bottle. It sailed through the air and arced down.

Hudson dodged to the side and it exploded on the pavement, splashing his pant leg with beer.

The skaters broke into howls of laughter and another round of threats and insults.

"Keep going," Cade whispered.

"Come around here again and you're dead!" Mohawk yelled.

They made it to the previous cross street and both jumped on their bikes. They turned and took off, for the first time in minutes remembering to breathe.

They continued on a while with Cade in the lead, doing his best to keep them headed east through a maze of streets that were anything but straight or straight forward.

Hudson eased up next to him. "Would you have really shot him?"

"Yeah."

Hudson's eyes went wide with surprise.

In the last twelve hours, the kid had been through hell. Nearly dying in the plane crash, losing his fiancé, and leaving his home for good.

It was a miracle that he wasn't curled up into a ball, crying his eyes out. Or worse, a hollowed out zombie stricken with shock. Maybe he was stronger than Cade first thought.

Or maybe so many things were constantly changing that there wasn't time to reflect on what had happened. They were in survival mode and that required total attention to the present moment.

Because they had no idea what was around the next corner. Nor the one after that.

The easy predictability of everyday life was slipping away.

And the journey had only just begun.

32

Sam slipped the Haltie onto Dennis' muzzle and fastened the strap around his neck. From long habit, he knew that meant they were going for a walk and he couldn't have been more excited. His back half was swinging back and forth along with his long destroyer of a tail.

Boxers usually got their tails clipped, but he was a mixed breed rescue and the organization they'd adopted him from hadn't done it for whatever reason.

Which suited Sam just fine.

Sure, it was long and heavy as a rope and was a constant danger to any glasses within swinging reach. A faded red wine stain on the couch was one casualty among many of his exuberant wagging.

But his tail was cute and it completed the sine wave of movement that ran through his body when he was excited.

She grabbed a couple of poo bags and stuffed them into her pocket. A couple because Dennis sometimes went for a surprise round two on longer walks.

She zipped up her lightweight jacket because mornings were always brisk in Durango. She'd be peeling off layers later when the summer sun burned through the morning chill.

Ethan sat at the breakfast table with a spoon in one hand and a graphic novel in the other. His eyes were glued to the pages while the spoon somehow scooped cereal into his mouth without spilling a drop of milk. His bony shoulders jutted out making it look like he didn't get enough food. Which couldn't have been more wrong because he was more or less always eating. Growing teenagers had gaping maws for mouths.

"Remember to shut off the generator after breakfast," she said.

He didn't respond.

She snapped her fingers in front of his face. "Earth to Ethan."

His eyes bounced to her like she'd appeared out of nowhere.

"The generator. Turn it off after you finish."

"Will do. You leaving?"

Hadn't they just gone over this a few minutes ago?

"Yes, Dennis needs a walk and I want to check on Grams."

"Give her a hug for me."

"I will, but you really need to go for a visit yourself. It's two miles away and you haven't been in a while."

"I know, I know. I will. I've just been busy with school and stuff."

"Well, you need to make time for your grandmother. She won't be with us forever."

"Okay, I will. Can you get off my back already? It's not like she remembers whether I came by or not anyway."

"Ethan!" Anger welled in Sam's chest and it was a feat that she didn't swear at him for being an insensitive idiot.

He cringed and knew he'd stepped in it. "Sorry."

"We'll discuss it later," Sam said before grabbing up the leash and stomping out the door with Dennis in tow. She started down the driveway and her day took another turn for the worse.

Her least favorite next-door neighbor was walking over. Had Brenda been waiting all morning to ambush her the second she went outside?

It was definitely possible.

Brenda met her at the end of the driveway. "Samantha, may I have a word with you?"

Sam suppressed an eye roll. It was better to get it over with because this woman never let anything go. "Sure, what?"

"A loud commotion woke me up in the middle of the night. And you know how much I need my sleep. I looked out the window to see who would be carrying on at such an hour and was disappointed to see you and Mr. Hensley were the culprits."

Commotion? Culprits?

They had had a brief conversation that at no point reached an unreasonable volume, and certainly never qualified as a commotion.

"Sorry about that," Sam said in a voice that she sincerely hoped her neighbor realized was completely insincere. She turned to leave.

"Well, what could be so important that you had to discuss it at that indecent hour?"

"Ask Gary." Sam tugged the leash and got into

stride. She smiled as she walked away because Brenda hated talking to Gary about anything because he didn't even pretend to be nice. The only thing Brenda hated worse than talking to Gary was other people knowing something she didn't.

Sam knew it was petty, but it still made her smile.

She and Dennis got into stride. She took a right on Arroyo and followed it down to Main. The route skirted along one end of the trailer park. She glanced up the street as she passed. Some kids were playing basketball. Nothing out of the ordinary.

After pausing for Dennis to do his business, she followed Main Ave north. Several stores were already open for business. More were in the process of opening their doors.

Sam waved at a few familiar faces in passing, but didn't stop for conversation. She was worried about Grams. This power outage or EMP or whatever it was meant the nursing home didn't have power and that worried her.

Why, exactly? She couldn't say.

She always worried about her mother. Worried if she was getting the care she needed. Worried if she was having a good day or a bad one. Worried if her own mother would know who she was the next time she saw her.

Fight the Shock

Parkinson's was a cruel way to go. It stole your essence before it finally took your life.

The walk helped. Getting her blood flowing and her lungs pumping always did. She turned right on Thirty-Second Street and crossed over the river that ran through the middle of town.

The Animas River was one of the things that made Durango such a special place. The blue-green water passed through a series of meandering oxbows to the north and then straightened out as it ran through the heart of town. It then continued south to the San Juan River and eventually fed into the mighty Colorado.

It was big enough to never go dry but still slow enough to offer abundant opportunities for recreation. Perfect for swimming, floating on tubes, fishing and more. It was the lifeblood of the community.

Some of her earliest memories were playing and splashing in the river with her parents. She and Cade had done the same thing with Lily and Ethan when they were old enough.

She waited for Dennis to sniff and pee on a signpost and then continued along Thirty-Second. She picked up the pace. The retirement home was a few blocks further and she was anxious to get there.

She looked both ways at the intersection and was about to cross when something caught her attention.

There was someone standing in the middle of the cross street wearing a blue robe and green slippers.

33

She recognized Mr. Ferguson when he turned around with a lost expression on his face. He was one of the residents at the retirement home. Her mother didn't like him much. She said he watched TV so loud she could hear it in her room at the end of the hall. And that he sometimes smelled bad. Sam regularly spent time at the home and had never personally experienced either of those issues with him. So she suspected there was something else behind the bad feelings.

Maybe her mother had asked for his chocolate pudding and he'd said no. It was probably something like that. Marjorie Bowman held onto grudges like they were gold nuggets to be guarded and treasured forever.

"Mr. Ferguson!" she called as she hurried over. She stopped in front of him while Dennis sniffed his legs up and down. "Mr. Ferguson, what are you doing out here?"

His clouded gaze sparked with recognition. "Samantha?"

"Yes, it's me."

"Thank goodness. I..." he looked around. "I don't know what happened. I got lost. I was walking through the gardens and then..."

The thought trailed off into nothing.

"How about I walk you home?"

He smiled. "That would be wonderful. I always tell Marjorie what a wonderful daughter you are."

"I try," Sam said as she hooked an arm through his and steered them in the right direction.

Thoughts swirled through Sam's head. All of them worrisome.

How had he wandered off with no one noticing?

Why had no one come looking for him?

What was going on at the retirement home for this to happen?

And the biggest one of all.

Was her mother okay?

It took longer than she wanted because Mr.

Ferguson couldn't move faster than a snail's slither. "Did you know I used to race cars back in the day?"

She knew.

Anyone that had ever spent more than a minute with him knew.

"Really?"

"Oh, yes." And he launched into a familiar story.

She listened and responded when prompted and they finally turned down the street to Sunshine Gardens Retirement Home. She let out a small sigh of relief. A part of her was expecting it be on fire or all the residents to be wandering around outside unattended.

But no. It looked like it always did.

From the outside, at least.

They followed the driveway up and she tied Dennis to a pole. She gave him a few scratches on the head. "Be back in a minute with some water."

He plopped down into a sit and licked Mr Ferguson's hand.

They entered the lobby of the main building. A young woman Sam didn't recognize was sitting at the reception desk. She glanced up as they arrived.

"Mr. Ferguson! Where have you been?" She circled around the desk and took his arm, and then glared at Sam "Who are you? Did you take him off the grounds without signing out?"

Sam almost exploded. "My name is Samantha Bowman. My mother, Marjorie Bowman, is a resident here."

"So why are you walking in with him then?"

Sam gritted her teeth and somewhat kept her cool. "Because I was walking over here to check on my mother and ran across Mr. Ferguson. He was standing in the middle of the street a few blocks away! All by himself and wondering how he'd gotten there!"

The woman cringed. "Really?"

"Yes, really! Who are you?"

"I'm Alice. I started last week. I'm sorry I snapped at you. I'm just exhausted. And freaking out a little."

"Why? What's going on?"

"It's the power outage last night. Only one person on the night shift showed up. And only me and Gabriella showed up this morning. She knows what she's doing but she's swamped. And Ms. Hopkins has gone MIA! Hasn't been seen since last night! We can't handle all these people by ourselves! I don't even know what I'm doing!"

Sam's anger melted as she felt the waves of panic

radiating off the poor girl. "It's going to be okay."

Mr. Ferguson pulled his arm away from Alice, his eyes suspicious. "Who are you? I don't know you."

"Let's all calm down and take a breath," Sam said. "Mr. Ferguson, this is Alice. She's new here and she's very nice. She's going to take you to your room." She turned to Alice. "Alice, did you know Mr. Ferguson used to race cars?"

Alice grinned. "I heard a rumor about that. Is it true?"

The old man's expression softened and he placed a hand over his heart. "On my honor, it is."

Alice mouthed thank you and guided him away.

Sam dashed down the hall, through the recreation room and turned into the wing to her mother's room. She skidded to a stop in front of an open door.

"Mom?" she said as she went inside. The bed with the patchwork quilt. The chair by the window that got flooded with light in the evening. The dresser in the corner with a TV on top. A black and white picture of her parents on their wedding day. Both of them smiling. So happy and young and ready for the life that had now passed. Reading glasses on the bedside table.

All the other things that Sam expected to see, but not her mother.

She started to panic.

What if she'd somehow wandered off too?

What if she'd gone further than Mr. Ferguson?

What if she'd made it to the river and fallen in?

Sam forced herself away from the edge. Just because her mother wasn't in the room didn't mean she'd met some horrible end.

Where could she be?

She wasn't in the recreation room.

There was one other place that she needed to check before she completely freaked out and turned this place upside down.

Sam raced into the hall and out the back door. She followed the path around the building, turned the corner, and exhaled.

Her mother was exactly where Sam usually found her when the weather was good. Sitting in her favorite chair next to her personal plot in the community garden. Garden gloves lying in the dark soil. An empty black plastic container from whatever she'd planted that morning.

She ran over and knelt in front of her. "Mom?"

Her mother opened her eyes and she smiled.

Good. She recognized her.

"Samantha?"

Sam cringed. She'd told her mother countless

times that she preferred Sam, but did she ever listen?

No.

It was always Samantha. And too often it was a reminder of how much she loved Bewitched and the lead character, whatever her real name was, who did the cutest little twitch of her nose whenever she wanted to do some magic. Well, having a baby girl was magic so she knew immediately what to name her.

Sam had never actually vomited from hearing the story yet again, but she'd come close.

"Did we have plans today?"

Sam fell into her arms and gave her a hug. "No, we didn't."

Her mother reciprocated the embrace and the tension flooded out of Sam's limbs.

She pulled back and wiped away a tear that had snuck out.

"Dear, are you okay? Did something happen? Did Ethan break another bone?"

Sam swallowed hard and pulled herself together. "No, he's fine."

"Is it Lily then? Did that boy do something to her?"

"No, mom. They broke up, and she dumped him. Remember?"

Her mother made a face. "He was always so nice. She could do worse, you know."

No one had told her about Colton's creepy behavior after the break up.

"We're all fine." It was a lie, but Sam couldn't handle anything else right now. "I was just worried about you. Did you know the power went out last night?"

"I heard about it this morning. Is it back on yet?"

Sam shook her head. "Not yet. I'm sure they'll have it fixed soon."

Another lie. She wasn't sure, but she did hope.

As much as she didn't want to believe it, she knew the truth. This wasn't a regular power outage. The walk through town proved that. All those cars left dead on the streets. Cade's truck just as useless. The TV and desktop computer at home that didn't come on when she plugged them into the generator that morning.

It was too much to be a coincidence. Too much by far.

But accepting that meant accepting something even worse. Lily and Cade were far away and she had no idea how they were doing.

34

Sitting in the dappled shade of a large oak tree, Cade finished an energy bar and gulped down some water to rehydrate. He and Hudson were far enough into the trees to not have to worry about being seen from the road at their backs. He watched the scene below with a strange mixture of amusement and pity.

The manicured grass of long fairways and oblong putting greens ran through the narrow valley. A group of golfers had just finished one hole and were walking to the next tee box. They puffed on cigars and an eruption of laughter carried over on the breeze. They gathered together at the next tee box and continued the jovial conversation.

Hudson snorted. "Just another day at the golf

course. How long do you think they're going to survive?"

It was the first time he'd spoken in a long while.

Cade gave a thin smile. "Don't know. But they're in for a rude awakening if they don't get with the program."

Hudson nodded agreement and they continued refueling their bodies while watching the spectacle.

They'd made it through Oakland without further incident and navigated the maze of twisty neighborhood streets that bordered Redwood Regional Park. From there, they'd turned south on Redwood Road and followed it through a vast stretch of forest-covered hills. They'd continued through the equally expansive Anthony Chabot Regional Park until arriving at its southern border.

Cade had called for a much-needed break, but it was time to get going again. He squinted up through the branches at the noonday sun and knew they were in for a scorcher with it being this hot already. He took another gulp of water and stashed the Camelbak into a bag strapped to the side of his bike. "How are you doing?"

Hudson had been pretty quiet since their run in with the skaters. Cade didn't mind the silence. He preferred it, actually. But he worried that it might mean the kid was starting to break down.

Hudson popped the last of an energy bar into his mouth and stood up. "Ready when you are."

Cade rose and laid a hand on his shoulder. "I mean, how are you holding up?"

"Oh," Hudson said with a frown. "I don't know. Okay, I guess. I don't think any of it feels real on some level. Like this is all just a dream, a nightmare, and I'm going through it but I know I'll wake up at some point and it will be over. You know?"

"Yeah, I do." He did. Only he also knew it wouldn't be over. Not if over meant going back to one second before the event.

Hudson's mouth twisted to the side and clearly something else was on his mind.

"What is it?"

Hudson pulled away and swung a leg over his bike. "It's those skaters. What right did they have to threaten us? Why couldn't they have just let us go by? We weren't bothering them."

"Some people are like that. They look for prey because they want something. Those guys weren't too serious."

"You should've shot Mr. Mohawk Tough Guy," he hissed. The venom in the words took Cade by surprise. "That would've shown the rest of those miscreants that we aren't prey."

"I told you, I would've if it had come to that. But I don't shoot people for insulting me."

"He threatened you."

"He did. But it was just words. It's better to defuse a situation if possible. If you go and turn every altercation into a gunfight, you're not going to survive for long."

"Whatever," Hudson replied as he kicked into the pedals and rode away.

Cade watched for a second before mounting his bike and following. What Hudson was feeling was normal. He'd been a victim several times in the last day. He didn't want to be one anymore. That was good. But swinging the pendulum all the way over to the other side wasn't. Going at everything with a guns-blazing Rambo style only worked in the movies.

They took Redwood Road south to interstate 580 and hooked a left onto the surface street that ran alongside.

Cade had to put all his focus on the ride because Hudson was hammering the pedals and setting a grueling pace. It wasn't one Cade could maintain forever, but he was happy to get through the mountain pass as fast as possible. He would've preferred not to take it at all, but it was that or waste half a day on one of the circuitous alternatives.

Eight exhausting miles later, the road sloped down toward the drab gray of the suburban town of Dublin. They went south on Foothill Rd toward Pleasanton. Cade had consulted his atlas on the rest stop and plotted a route that would take them around the edges of Pleasanton and Livermore. It was country roads for the most part. They'd eventually end up on Patterson Pass Road and take that through another range of squat mountains that ran perpendicular to their path.

They'd gone a ways when Hudson's frenetic pace slowed. Cade pulled up alongside him and saw the reason for it. A wide flat area tucked into a nook in the foothills had a swarm of activity going on. It was too far to make out the details, but Cade had an idea of what it was.

"Come on," Cade said as he steered his bike off the road and down the slope on the opposite side. They walked their bikes a while as the sounds of bustling activity grew louder. He found a thicket of scrub brush and they stowed their bikes inside. "I'm going to take a look." He dug out his binoculars and scrambled up the slope to the road.

Peering under a guardrail, he glassed the scene.

Dozens of soldiers were building a perimeter of chain link fence. Others were erecting temporary structures in what would eventually be the interior. A convoy of military transport trucks in the distance turned off the road. A plume of dust rose behind them as they crossed over a span of unpaved land before coming to a stop next to a gathering of other vehicles.

And then he saw it.

A cluster of shipping container offices.

One had big block letters painted on the side.

FEMA

The Federal Emergency Management Agency was putting down roots and judging by the sheer volume of soldiers and vehicles involved, they were going to stay a while.

35

Cade scooted back down the embankment and joined Hudson in the cover of the scratchy brush.

"What is it?"

"Looks like a FEMA camp going up."

"FEMA camp? What's that?"

"The Federal Emergency Management Agency. Looks like they're setting up a base of operations to coordinate a response in the local area. Offer refuge to those who need it. That kind of thing."

"That sounds good. We should ask them to help us."

Cade shook his head. "No."

"Why not?"

"Because it might not end there. Some folks say

they're going to imprison Americans and take away our rights."

"What? Why would they do that?"

"I'm not saying they are. I don't know what they plan on doing and I'm not going to find out."

"It's our government. Their job is to help us."

Cade gave it a second because he wasn't sure if the kid was joking or not.

He wasn't.

"Look, even if you're right and all they want to do is help, their idea of helping could be very different from our idea of helping. And the problem with that is that by the time we found out, it could be too late to change our minds. What if they designate us as refugees and don't let us leave?"

That got Hudson thinking.

"There's going to be a lot of people trying to get some place in the coming days. Once they realize this isn't a temporary emergency and the government isn't going to fix everything, they're going to take matters into their own hands. And that means a lot of desperate people on the move. FEMA will want to control that."

Hudson nodded.

"Whatever their intentions, I have to get to my

daughter. So, if you want to go ask for help, this is where we part ways."

"I'm with you. Better to steer clear."

Cade checked the map and plotted a new route that cut east towards town a ways and then back south to continue on as before. They headed out and he was glad to put some distance between them and whatever was brewing back there.

Hudson slipped into a sullen silence, but fortunately stuck to a more moderate pace this time.

They rode along country roads and, aside from the infrequent vehicle stopped in the road, there wasn't much that hinted at the unfolding disaster.

They made it to Patterson Pass Road and took a right to head east. They hadn't gone far when the sound of gunshots erupted.

Cade smashed on the handbrakes and steered off the road down the steep embankment. The front tire hit the bottom of the drainage ditch and he somehow managed to keep from flying over the handlebars. That wasn't to say he didn't wipeout. He did.

But it was a semi-controlled wipeout so he and the bike hit the dirt without suffering major damage.

Another burst of gunfire.

Hudson skidded to a stop and looked over his shoulder.

"Get down!" Cade yelled as he pulled the shotgun out of a side bag. He pulled out his pistol and chamber-checked that it was ready to fire.

Hudson dropped down beside him.

They clawed up the gravel slope and peeked down the road.

An old farm truck was coming their way, weaving back and forth across the road. One of the big ones with high plywood sides in the back that were used to haul produce. A ways behind it was a souped up, early seventies Cutlass Supreme. Copper paint and wide tires. A figure leaned out the window and fired at the truck.

One of the bullets must've hit the truck's front tire because it exploded and the truck veered out of control. It swerved over to the edge, then overcorrected to the opposite side and finally screeched sideways and came to a stop fifty feet away from Cade and Hudson.

The Cutlass kicked out to the side and stopped. Three guys jumped out and ducked behind the car for cover.

The truck's door flew open and a farmer hopped

out with a vintage Western style rifle in hand. He crouched behind the hood and waited.

One of the guys yelled. "Give us the money, old man! Do it now and we'll let you go!"

The farmer popped up and fired a shot over the hood.

A hail of gunfire came back, thudding into the thick metal panels of the truck. They had AR-15s and knew how to use them. Another burst of fire and bullets pinged off the hood.

"You're outgunned! And if you shoot at my ride again, there'll be no walking away!"

The farmer peeked over the hood and fired.

Glass shattered and one of the guys cursed.

A storm of fire came back, chewing up the side of the truck but not one round punched through. It was fifties era craftsmanship and solid like a tank.

Cade didn't know how this thing had started, but he knew how it would end. The farmer wasn't going to make it. It was sad and it was wrong, but it was reality.

If they kept their heads down and kept quiet, they could sneak off and follow the ditch away.

He was about to tell Hudson the plan when the kid spoke first.

"We have to help him."

"No, we don't."

"Yes, we do! Those guys are going to kill him!"

Hudson started to rise.

Cade let go of the shotgun, grabbed a fistful of shirt and shoved him back down. "Stay down! This isn't our fight! The only thing trying to help that poor man will do is get us killed too!"

"So it's just like with the skaters then, huh? Run away and let the bad guys win again!"

"It's called staying alive. As much as I'd like to help, my first priority is staying alive so I can get to my daughter."

"You're a coward!"

Cade fought the anger growing in his belly. The kid was mixed up and lashing out. He blew out a hard breath.

"I'm not running away this time!" Hudson snatched the shotgun and twisted out of Cade's grasp. He dashed up the slope and sprinted away.

The farmer saw him coming and raised his rifle.

"I'm here to help you!" Hudson yelled with the shotgun held out to the side.

The AR-15s let off another burst and the idiot kid was lucky not to get his head blown off.

He ducked into cover beside the farmer and told

him something. He pointed back at Cade and the farmer looked over.

The farmer waved.

Cade stayed low and slunk back down the embankment. He could leave right now and the kid would die too. He chewed on that and didn't like the taste.

If he was going to get involved, he wasn't going to run over and wait until they all got shot to pieces. If he was going to even consider it, there had to be a better way. Something that shifted the odds into their favor.

And then he saw it.

"Dammit," he hissed.

36

A drainage culvert ran under the road twenty feet away. It would be a tight squeeze, but it looked big enough to get through. An almond orchard on the other side of the road would provide cover for Cade to sneak by the bad guys and then take them by surprise from behind.

If something didn't go wrong.

And, of course, any number of things could go wrong because that's how life worked. It was just more obvious in those moments when a single mistake could turn out to be fatal.

Cade ejected the magazine and verified it was full. He palmed it back in and crawled over to the culvert. Puddles of stale brown water filled the valleys of the ridged pipe. A bright circle of light spilled in from the other side. It wasn't that far, but it was smaller than he'd expected.

He ducked his head inside and his shoulders bumped into the edges of the pipe. He tried again with both arms extended out and just managed to squeeze in. He drove his boots into the gravel and had to wriggle like a worm once his whole body was inside. He inched forward, his toes and hands working together to lift and push in unison.

He'd made it halfway through when the diameter of the pipe changed imperceptibly. To his eyes anyway. Not to his body. It squeezed on his shoulders. Another heave but he didn't move an inch. He tried to go back but that didn't work either.

He was stuck and couldn't fill his lungs all the way because there wasn't room.

Panic roiled in his gut. A wild electric edge that fought to take over and leave him senseless. The thought of getting stuck in there for good filled his mind. He couldn't call out for help. That would get him killed. But what was the alternative?

A slow and agonizing death from dehydration and exposure.

He blew out a slow, shallow breath and pushed down the fear. Losing it wasn't going to help.

Another breath and he tried the only thing he could think of.

He took a few breaths to get oxygen into his system and then blew the last one out. And kept blowing. More than a normal exhale. He kept blowing until his lungs emptied out and his chest ached with the need for another breath.

The pressure on his shoulders eased a fraction and he kicked forward with his toes. It was enough. He squeezed through the tight spot and the diameter returned to a still claustrophobic constriction.

But it was manageable.

He inched through the remainder and made it out the other side.

A part of him wanted to rethink the whole thing, but that meant going back through the culvert and there was no way he was doing that again.

Cade kept low and hustled into the trees a ways before hooking right and going parallel to the road.

The firefight had quieted down but he had no illusions about it being over.

The bad guys were planning their next move. Or waiting for the farmer and Hudson to show enough of themselves to present a proper target.

He darted from one row of trees to the next, glancing toward the road in the open spaces between. He finally spotted the Cutlass and dove into the next row of trees, certain they'd seen him and that a volley of deadly fire was coming his way.

But no.

They hadn't.

He continued through two more rows and then cut back toward the road. He made it to the embankment and edged up to take a look.

All three were lined up behind the Cutlass, attention and weapons focused down the road. One turned around and Cade ducked just in time.

Their voices floated over to him.

"We gotta kill those bastards. I'm not going to sit here all day twiddling my thumbs, waiting for them to run out of ammo."

"Now you're talking! Should we rush them all at once?"

"Yeah, sure, if you want to die, idiot. No, we're going to be smart. See the embankments on both sides? One of you is going to sneak down each side and take them by surprise. I'll keep their attention up here on the road."

Cade cursed.

Any second, one of them was going to walk over and see him pitched over on the slope. It was now or never.

He crept up just enough to get a clear shot. He lined up the sights on the closest one and squeezed off two rounds.

Both hit center mass and the guy slumped against the car.

The other two reacted faster than him and his next shots missed as one dove into the car and the other disappeared on the other side of the road.

Cade fired a few rounds into the driver's door, but didn't know if any had gone through.

The Cutlass' engine roared and it fishtailed around. The tires screeched and smoked as it took off like a rocket.

The guy hidden in the opposite ditch ran up onto the road, yelling and cursing at being left behind.

Cade was lining up the front sight when a rifle shot went off.

The guy took one in the back and fell to the pavement.

The farmer was leaning over the hood. He fired again and another round found its mark.

Cade finished off the first guy and turned to do the same to the other, but he was already dead. He watched the Cutlass speed away and finally took a breath.

He gathered up their rifles and found extra magazines in their jackets. He was rummaging through their pockets when Hudson and the farmer arrived. He pocketed what was useful and left the rest.

He rose to find the farmer's hand extended toward him. "My name's Wesley Guthrie and I believe I owe you my life. Thank you."

Cade shook his hand and got a good look at him for the first time.

Late sixties. Early seventies. Thin white hair parted on the side. His face lined with deep wrinkles that were crusted with dirt. Skin like leather. A checkered long sleeve shirt with the cuffs rolled up. Faded denim jeans with patches sewn over the knees. Clear blue eyes that didn't miss a thing.

"Cade Bowman. Glad it worked out like it did."

He didn't have to add that it could've gone another way and ended up with them dead on the road instead.

"Yeah, me too."

Hudson grinned. "I knew we'd kick their asses!"

Cade stifled the urge to slap him. They were going to have a serious conversation about it. But now wasn't the time.

"You folks from around here?" Wesley asked.

"No. Home is Durango, but we're heading to Las Vegas."

"Long way to go on foot."

"We've got bikes over in the ditch," Hudson said. "What did those guys want from you?"

"What else? Money. I just dropped off a full load of organic heirloom tomatoes to my distributor in Livermore. Those lowlifes must've known about it somehow."

Hudson pulled a face. "You accepted payment in cash?"

Wesley frowned. "Yeah, not smart in hindsight. But I've always done it that way and never had a problem before. Was making my peace with the Lord when you folks showed up."

He eyed the two AR-15s slung over Cade's shoulder. "Nice score there."

Cade wondered if he was going to ask for one and then wondered further how he would answer.

"Anyhow, I'm heading home to Elderwood. It's a speck of a town northeast of Visalia. Not even a post office since the local branch closed twenty years ago. Be happy to give you a ride. It'll get you halfway to Vegas a lot faster than a bicycle."

It wasn't part of the original plan.

It was better.

It was an unexpected opportunity. The kind Cade hoped they'd run across but knew they couldn't count on.

But here it was.

And he couldn't have been more thankful.

"Thank you. That would be amazing. My legs are about to fall off from riding all day."

37

The trip back to Wesley's farm took a good six hours because they stuck to country roads and went out of their way to avoid Modesto, Merced and Fresno. The rose glow of twilight was fading into the darker blues of night when the farm finally came into view.

The sound of dogs barking greeted them as they pulled off the dirt road and onto the dirt tracks that led to the house.

Wesley turned on the headlights. The bright beams revealed dozens of dogs racing toward them. The whole pack twisting and jumping and leaping around and over each other.

Hudson stiffened and his mouth dropped open.

Wesley chuckled. "Don't worry. They're tame, for the most part. As long as they see you're a friend, you've got nothing to worry about." He slowed the truck as the dogs gathered round, barking and yelping their heads off.

Cade flinched away as one leaped up and appeared in the side window for an instant. He loved dogs more than most. Grown up with them. Always had at least one in his life. But this was crazy. "Do you operate a rescue center on the side?"

Wesley laughed. "Not officially. But you could say that. I take in strays and dogs that the pound is going to put down. Some haven't worked out, but most find their place in the pack and do fine. I even adopt one out from time to time, so long as I know it's going to a good home."

"How much do you charge?" Hudson asked.

"Nothing."

"Nothing? It costs five hundred dollars to adopt a dog in San Francisco."

"And people still do it?"

"Oh, yeah. All the time. My fiancé and I..." he trailed off.

Wesley looked over and Cade shook his head.

They pulled up to a white, two-story clapboard farmhouse with a wide porch out front. Mismatched chairs and side tables beside the screened front door. A porch swing that wasn't quite level on the far end. Floral patterned curtains hung in the windows. A line of metal bowls on the ground along the edge of the house. A wiry-haired Jack Russell mix darted from bowl to bowl, sniffing inside each for a forgotten morsel.

A barn and other outbuildings surrounded the house. Fields in various stages of harvest surrounded it all.

Wesley killed the engine but left the lights on. "You mind helping me feed this ravenous pack? If they don't get properly full, they might come after us in our sleep."

Hudson's eyes went wide.

Wesley elbowed him good-naturedly. "I'm joshing. They won't come after me."

Hudson's eyes darted to Cade for confirmation.

"He's kidding," Cade said and he was pretty sure it was true.

Wesley climbed out and made the introductions.

The pack sniffed over Cade and he gave the ones that came close a pat for greeting. They quickly turned their attention to Hudson, likely picking up on his nervous energy.

"Is this okay? Is this what they normally do?" Hudson said when a beagle hopped up and started humping his leg.

Wesley pushed it off. "Elvira! Behave yourself!"

Elvira darted away, her tail wagging furiously.

They waded through a mass of fur and bumping bodies, up the steps to the porch. Wesley shooed them away and the three slipped inside. Together, they helped fill all the bowls and fed the impatient mob. The howling and barking and yelping finally quieted down because food was more enticing than visitors.

Though Elvira kept looking over at Hudson, making him nervous.

Finally, the last bowl was filled and all the dogs were busy eating. All except for one. A cute little auburn-colored dachshund that had stuck to Wesley's heel and ignored the other dogs like they weren't worth so much as a sniff. Something was wrong with her back leg because she had a pronounced limp.

Wesley scooped it up and tucked it under his arm. "This is Lottie. Found her half-dead on the road after getting hit by a car. Took her to the vet and they did what they could, but she'll never be the same." He stroked her long muzzle. "For some reason, she's gotten it into her head that she's the queen around here."

She barked and he nuzzled her ear. "Oh, you hush." He turned up the steps and they followed.

Cade laughed. "I think I see why she thinks that."

Wesley chuckled and led them inside to a small kitchen. He set Lottie on the floor and she resumed her position at his heel. He lit a couple of lanterns for light and started pulling things out of the fridge and cabinets. "I imagine you folks are as hungry as I am. Let's pile up some plates and go take a seat on the porch."

After Cade filled his plate with two pork chops, mashed potatoes, corn on the cub with a fat slice of butter and coated with salt, green beans, fried okra, a scoop of dressing, and collard greens, he paused to admire the mountain of delicious food.

And then felt a little self-conscious.

Wesley must've noticed because he laughed. "Don't be shy. Eat up. I won't be able to finish all this myself."

He didn't feel so bad when he saw that Hudson's plate was just as full.

"Save room though," Wesley said. "Ms. Whitley brought by some of her world famous rhubarb pie yesterday. You will not want to miss out on that. I promise you."

"I don't know how to thank you for all this, for letting us stay the night," Cade said.

"It's me who should be thanking you. I wouldn't be looking forward to a slice of that pie without your help."

Wesley led them out to the porch and they brought the lanterns along.

Hudson jumped when glowing eyes reflected back from the bottom step.

The dogs that had finished their dinners were gathered round the bottom step, but not coming up.

Cade and Hudson took a seat and were about to dig in when Wesley interrupted.

"You mind if I say a blessing first?"

"Not at all," Cade said.

Wesley finished the prayer and then the conversation went quiet while they tore into the feast. All that could be heard was the tinking of forks on porcelain plates and the occasional whine from one of the dogs waiting more or less patiently below.

Lottie sat in Wesley's lap and got a nibble of about every fifth bite that Wesley took for himself. She was definitely queen of the manor.

Once they'd plowed through an indecent amount of food and their bellies were uncomfortably bloated, conversation picked up again. They hadn't talked much on the ride over because the farm truck's old diesel engine made shouting the only way to be heard. But they had discussed the event and Cade had explained what they were most likely facing.

"An EMP, huh?" Wesley said as he poked at the last few green beans on his plate. "Guess that means we're at war."

"Most likely, yes," Cade said.

"Who attacked us?"

"My guess is North Korea or Iran. Whoever did it is now a smoking pile of irradiated ash."

"How?" Hudson said. "I thought the EMP toasted almost everything."

"We have fourteen Ohio-class submarines patrolling the waters around the world. They carry about half of our active strategic thermonuclear warheads. Besides those, some portion of the domestic military apparatus will have survived the pulse. The military has known about the EMP threat for years. They know how to harden infrastructure and vehicles to withstand an EMP. It's just been a matter of budget dollars and priorities to get it done." He turned to Hudson. "You saw all those military vehicles outside Pleasanton. A lot of them looked vintage, probably pulled out of mothballs from a local National Guard armory. But plenty more were newer models that must've been hardened."

Wesley tossed a few bones off the porch and the scramble below made clear the dogs had been waiting for it.

Cade left a few good bits of meat on his pork chops and lobbed them out to the pack.

Crickets chirped and a bullfrog trumpeted his mating call. A breeze rustled through the leaves of the towering elm on the side of the house. The heat of the day had broken. The cool air a relief on skin made pink by the sun.

It was idyllic.

A peaceful little corner of the world.

But for how much longer?

38

Lily shifted position to relieve the ache in her shoulders. It helped, a little. She and Piper had been tied up and sitting on that filthy couch all day long.

The light filtering through the sheets covering the windows was fading so the sun must've dipped below the horizon. It had been nothing but hours and hours of waiting. Waiting while her imagination ran wild with all the horrible things that would happen to them.

It had been so long that Donny had gotten drunk, stomped around ranting about Zeke double-crossing him and how he was going to kill the traitor, threatened to knock Lily's head off, ran out of beer, finally sobered up, decided Zeke would never do that after all they'd been through together, eaten something that looked like it hadn't been edible in days, smoked a bowl of meth, jittered around again threatening to beat the crap out of them, come down and been angry there wasn't any more beer, and finally, half an hour ago, fallen asleep. He sat in a ratty brown recliner across the room. One leg hanging over the side. Chin resting on his chest and snoring. The revolver that he'd waved in their faces all day long in his lap. One hand near it, but not holding it.

It was now or never.

As soon as Zeke got back, they'd be taken to whoever Jax was and he sounded even worse than these two.

Lily rolled back on the couch and bumped into Piper.

Piper jerked away. "What?"

"Shhh," Lily said. She rolled back into a ball and reached her bound hands out. With a little work, she managed to squeeze her legs through her arms and end up with her hands in front. The change from having them behind her for the last however many hours brought a measure of instant relief to her aching shoulders.

"What are you doing?" Piper whispered.

Lily held her finger up to her lips. She wrenched

her arms out trying to snap the three zip ties cinched around her wrists. They didn't break. They did cut into her skin though, almost making her cry out.

It would've been better to have them off, but it wasn't required.

She carefully lowered herself to the floor.

A spring in the couch creaked and she froze.

Waiting for Donny to wake up and come flying at her in a rage.

His snoring continued without a hitch.

Lily got on all fours because she couldn't walk with the zip ties around her ankles.

"No," Piper hissed. "Don't do it. He'll kill us."

Lily started toward him. And more specifically, toward the handgun in his lap. If she could get it without waking him up, this whole nightmare could end. More importantly, the nightmare yet to come could be averted.

She scooted along, closing the distance inches at a time. She set her hands down on something she hadn't seen. A cellophane wrapper crinkled. In the relative quiet, it sounded like a car alarm going off.

She froze, too scared to even breathe.

Donny's snores stuttered and he shifted in the chair. His head tipped to the side. The hand by the gun scratched himself. He muttered something and she knew it was over.

But then he settled and the snoring returned to a regular rhythm.

She let out the breath and took another to steady her nerves. She continued forward, getting closer.

A car outside sped up the street. Louder as it approached.

Fear flooded through her and settled in her belly with a sickening splash.

Zeke was back.

They were going to be taken to Jax. A criminal underlord that dabbled in the sex slave trade from what she'd heard.

Headlights flooded through the front window, lighting up the living room. The car roared by. Light swept across the wall, hit Donny and slid away. The car roared down the street.

Whoever it was, it wasn't Zeke.

Donny's eyelids fluttered and he shifted again. The gun fell off his lap and into the crease between his leg and the chair.

Lily gritted her teeth. She looked around, thinking maybe she should grab something to hit him with.

But nothing obvious was nearby.

She glanced at her bag on the kitchen counter. Donny had rummaged through it earlier in the day and the contents lay scattered everywhere. He'd even found her room key with the room number written on the back. She'd thought writing the number on it had been a smart move in case they forgot. It felt differently when he flashed in front of their faces, talking about visiting the room later.

There was nothing in the bag that would help because he'd taken her pocket knife.

So, it had to be his gun.

She had to get it.

She edged forward and made it to the chair. The rank stink of his sour sweat overpowering at this distance. She brought her knees forward and straightened up. She reached toward the crease where the gun had to be.

Donny's eyes snapped open. He kicked out and caught her in the chest before she could react.

She tumbled backward and smacked her head on the carpet.

He grabbed the gun and jumped up. "What are you doing? What are you doing?" He jabbed the gun at her. "You think I won't kill you? You think I won't do it? I will put a hole in your head! I will leave you dying in a gutter!"

But he didn't shoot.

She was his way out. She was the merchandise and she wasn't worth anything dead.

"Were you trying to get my gun? You little whore!"

Lily pushed up and shook her head. "No, I was trying to wake you up. I kept telling you to wake up, but you wouldn't."

His suspicious eyes didn't soften. "Why were you doing that?"

"We need to pee. We've been holding it all day."

It was true and the best lies always had a bit of truth in them.

He scowled. "I should just let you piss your pants."

"Do you want to take us to Jax smelling like urine?"

He glared at her. "Don't be trying to tell me how to run my business!"

"I'm not, but I do have to pee."

He made a face, but waved the gun toward the slider door to the backyard. "Fine. Whatever. I'll take you one at a time."

Lily pointed at the zip ties pinning her ankles together. "I'm not going to be able to pee like this. Girls squat, in case you didn't know."

"Shut up, smartass!" He pulled out a pocketknife and whipped the blade open.

Lily leaned back and pushed her feet out.

"You go last. Piss yourself for all I care."

He went over to Piper and cut her ankles free. He yanked her up and marched her out to the backyard. He stood in the entrance, his eyes bouncing from the backyard to the living room to keep tabs on both of them. A minute later, Piper returned.

"Do we have to do the ankle ones? They hurt and my swollen feet are killing me."

"They hurt," he said in a baby voice. "Wah. Cry me a river." He dragged her to the couch and threw her down. He cinched down another three zip ties around her ankles and she winced.

"You don't want it to cut her ankles up," Lily said. "Jax won't like it if we have skin peeling off."

Donny shoved Piper's feet away and grinned like a shark. "Jax ain't going to be checking out that part of your body."

Her belly squirmed with fear and disgust. He didn't say which parts were going to be checked out.

But he didn't have to.

39

Donny sliced the zip ties off Lily's ankles. He wasn't the least bit careful about it and nicked the thin skin on the bone in the process.

She forced herself to not react. She didn't want to give him the satisfaction.

He yanked her up, nearly pulling her shoulder out of the socket. He shoved her outside and made a face. "Let's go, Spice. Do your business and make it quick."

Lily looked around for a way out. A six foot stockade fence surrounded a small yard. Half the yard was taken up by a small rectangular pool. No water except for the scummy water in the deep end. The odor from the pool hit her and she gagged.

It was an open sewer.

Donny laughed. "This ain't no five star hotel, princess. Just hang your butt off the edge and get it over with."

Lily shot him a look and then searched for a better option. Anything would qualify. There was a round plastic table and chairs. The kind every cheap hotel had out by the pool. The kind that didn't matter much if they got stolen.

Which was probably how these ended up here.

"Are you going to stand there and watch?"

Donny grinned and the look confirmed he was going to do exactly that.

"You're sick."

"You don't know the half of it. But maybe you'll find out."

She walked around the table and flipped it on its side. She squatted down behind it and did her business. She really did have to pee. But she also took the opportunity to continue searching for a way out.

There was a gate on the side of the house. But an interior door had been nailed across it to seal it shut.

"Spice is feeling bashful all of a sudden. How cute. Now finish up or I'll drag you back inside with pee running down your legs!"

She'd already finished.

There was no easy way out. She was going to have to jump the fence. If she ran to the corner, she could put a left foot on the lower rail, hook her bound hands over the top, push off the opposite corner with her right foot and hopefully scramble over before he could stop her.

It would mean leaving Piper behind. But if she didn't try to escape, neither of them had a chance. She had no doubt that she could outrun Donny. Running fifty feet would probably send him into spasms of coughing. All she had to do was get over the fence and run.

"Hey!" Donny yelled and started over.

She took off at a sprint.

Leaped into position, left foot on the rail and hands grabbing hold of the pointed top, right foot to the side to get traction off the corner.

And her shoe went straight through the rotten wood.

Instead of vaulting over the top, she slammed into the fence and bounced off with her leg caught at the knee in the fence. She yanked it out and was about to try again, but was too late.

Her head snapped back.

She screamed for help as loud as she could.

Donny had a fistful of her hair. He jerked again

and she fell over backward. He kicked her in the stomach.

A flash of pain shot through her middle. She groaned and doubled over on her side.

Donny pulled back for another kick but stopped. "You try something like that again and I will kill you! Forget the money! Forget it all! I will gut you like a pig. I will pull out your intestines and shove them in your mouth until you choke to death!"

He stood over her, screaming with rage. The screaming went on a little longer, until he ran out of breath or threats to make. There clearly was no one within shouting distance that would help them. Or else he wouldn't have carried on that loud and that long.

And then he went quiet and it got worse.

He unzipped his pants. He stood above her, fondling himself. After a minute, he cursed and zipped back up. "You're so damn ugly I can't even get hard." He spat on her.

Fury and humiliation burned in her chest. She never would've believed anyone could treat another person like that. It was then that she started to lose hope. Not all of it and not all at once. But that was the first moment where real doubt stabbed like a splinter into her heart.

What if she and Piper didn't get away?

What if their future was one she couldn't imagine living?

Donny dragged her up. He shoved her toward the slider door. "Not feeling so Spicy now, are you?"

He pushed her inside and threw her down next to Piper. He zip tied her ankles together, making sure they pinched tight, then went to the kitchen.

"What happened?"

Lily didn't answer. She didn't want to talk. She didn't want to be. She shook her head and pulled her knees into her chest. She wanted to curl up like a rollie pollie and leave only a hard shell facing the outside world.

But she couldn't.

So she dropped her head and tried to disappear into the mildewy cushions.

40

Minutes dragged by and each one dragged Lily deeper into a hole of misery. After Donny finally nodded off, Piper whispered to her asking if she was okay. She didn't answer.

She wasn't okay.

None of this was okay.

If it wasn't so horribly real, she would've pinched herself and struggled to awake from the nightmare. Surely, she was in bed in the Mandalay. She'd wake up and the sun would be shining in the window with the promise of an extravagant all-you-can-eat buffet downstairs. They'd eat themselves into a stupor, gorge until the last fork full of pancake was stuffed down. Then they'd tour the aquariums because they hadn't done it yet and that had been the whole point of staying there.

Piper claimed to love sea life. She did. It was true. She just loved it on the other side of a thick pane of safety glass. She'd gone to Miami with her family last year and posted a zillion gorgeous pictures of the beaches and blue water. Her posts went on and on about the ocean and how amazing it was. You never would've known from the posts that she never once dipped a single toe in the water. She didn't even like to walk on the wet sand after the tide sucked back into the sea.

There were too many squishy things that got left behind.

None of that mattered though because this wasn't a dream and so waking up wasn't an option.

The sound of a car engine grew louder, louder still as headlights flashed through the dark room. It didn't pass by this time. The garage door clanked and rolled open.

The noise jolted Donny awake. He jumped up and peeked behind the sheet to see out the front window. "Zeke, that better be you, man."

He hustled to the kitchen and hid behind the fridge. He aimed his gun at the door to the garage and waited. "Zeke," he muttered, but the rest was too low to make out.

The garage door clanged and banged shut. A few seconds later, the door to the kitchen door creaked and started to open.

A gunshot split the air.

The door slammed shut.

"Jesus!" Zeke yelled from the garage. "It's me, man!"

"Zeke?"

"Yes, you idiot!"

Donny opened the door, still holding the pistol and flashlight in front. The beam hit Zeke right in the face.

He covered up with an arm. "It's me already!" He pushed Donny to the side and stomped into the kitchen. "You could've killed me! What the hell is wrong with you?"

"It was an accident. Come on. I'm sorry. You took so long I was thinking it didn't go well. Like, what if Jax didn't like the offer and cut off your nuts and made you give up our address? That could've been a squad of trained assassins coming to take me out, man!"

Zeke ran a hand over his face. "Are you serious?"

"Yeah."

"A squad of trained assassins?"

"It could happen."

"You think Jax believes it would take a squad of trained assassins to kill you?"

"Whatever, man! Don't get stuck on the details. My God. The point is that it could've been someone here to kill me. That's why I was jumpy."

Zeke tossed the keys on the counter and brushed past. Tried to, rather, because Donny grabbed his jacket and spun him around.

"So?"

"We got any beer?"

"Don't give me that. What did he think of my offer?"

"*Your* offer? Don't you mean *our* offer?"

"Yeah, of course. Damn, you're touchy tonight."

"Well, you nearly killed me and then half-blinded me with that stupid flashlight. And that's after I had to wait all day long to finally get a two minute meeting with Jax. So, yeah. I'm cranky." He grabbed inside the beer carton and came up empty. "You drank all the beer?"

"What did Jax say? Do we have a deal or not?"

Zeke's scowl melted into a grin. "He's interested. He said the girls better be worth it or else he'll cut both our nuts off and bury us alive in the desert." He swallowed hard. "He wasn't bluffing."

"I told you about the nuts part! Didn't I?"

"That doesn't mean you were right about the assassins."

Piper scooted closer to Lily. Her body trembled and she was crying quietly.

Lily found her hand and squeezed. It was all the reassurance she had to offer and even that was fake. Being talked about like possessions, like goods to be bought and sold, had her standing on the edge of a cliff with a bottomless, black void below.

And with every passing minute, she inched closer to falling in.

Donny passed Zeke a mostly empty bottle of booze. "So when's the meeting and where?"

Zeke took a few gulps of the clear liquid and then hissed from the burn. "Tomorrow evening at the compound."

"You mean his personal place?"

Zeke nodded.

"Seriously?"

"Yep."

Donny leaped up and clapped. "Yes! This is it! This is where it all begins. I told you, buddy. We're going big time, baby. No more nickel and dime crap. See what I mean? Think big and big things happen."

"Yeah, I just hope that big thing isn't us getting killed."

Donny slapped him on the shoulder. "Don't be such a downer. He's not going to whack people in his own house. That would attract unwanted attention. He's smart. That's why he wants to do business with us."

"I hope you're right."

"I am right! I've been right this whole time! Hey, did you get a little something to celebrate?"

Zeke's brow arched. "What are you talking about?"

Donny grabbed at his jacket pockets, but Zeke pulled away.

"He gave us some on the house. He said it was a goodwill gesture for business partners." Zeke pulled a baggie out of his pocket and dangled it in front of Donny's face.

Donny got the pipe and lighter and they were both cranked up a few minutes later.

Lily squeezed her eyes shut. She'd seen enough. She'd seen too much.

Unfortunately, this wasn't a bad dream and she couldn't wake up to make it go away.

41

The end of the day had finally arrived and Sam couldn't wait to get off her feet. She'd spent a good ten hours helping out at the retirement home because most of the staff hadn't shown up for work. She was used to hard work. Being a fifth grade teacher wasn't exactly a cake walk. Especially not with new budget cuts constantly chipping away at the school's finances. Annual fundraising had become almost as big a part of her job as teaching the kids.

But helping elderly people all day long was in another league entirely. For starters, they were a lot bigger than fifth graders and some of them needed a lot more help.

She wouldn't forget the bed pans. Not for a long time.

She crossed her arms behind her back and squeezed. A cascade of satisfying cracks pulsed along her spine. She blew out an exhale of relief. Her back muscles were going to be hurting tomorrow. Ice packs would've been nice, but they were needed to help keep the freezer cold overnight. With no power and the generator shut down until morning, keeping the freezer at the correct temperature until morning was vital. Losing hundreds of dollars worth of groceries wasn't an option.

Especially since she hadn't been able to go shopping again that day. If this was an EMP and other people understood the situation, the local grocery stores were going to be wiped out in no time. She'd have to go in the morning and add to their pantry of non-perishables.

As part of his dedication to being prepared, Cade had long ago stocked up months of emergency rations. Along with a large amount of non-perishables in the pantry, they would be better off than most.

Still, if this was an EMP attack, they were going to need more. The way Cade had described the aftermath of such an attack was almost too terrifying to believe. He'd probably overstated the danger so she wouldn't complain about him spending what little extra money they had on being prepared.

She'd hounded him about it any number of times. She regretted doing that now. If this was the real deal, they were going to need every bit of food and gear to survive the months ahead.

But first, her family needed to get home. She hadn't heard from Lily or Cade and so had no idea where they were or how they were doing. The worry ate her up inside. That had been the one blessing of working so hard all day long. She'd been too busy to think about anything else.

She went around the house with a flashlight, making sure that the doors and windows were locked. She paused at Ethan's closed door. Light seeped into the hallway from the crack underneath. She started to knock but stopped herself.

She wanted to apologize. Needed to after coming down too hard on him at dinner. But it wasn't all her fault. She'd had a rough day and was in no mood for attitude about helping out. He probably needed more time to cool down. She decided to give him some space and extend an olive branch before going to bed.

She descended the half-set of stairs and checked

the front door. The kitchen and garage next. She checked and locked the sliding door to the backyard and was closing the blinds when she remembered the generator outside.

Gary had come by earlier that day and told Ethan about another neighbor having their generator stolen right out of their backyard.

What was happening to their neighborhood? It had always been such a safe and friendly place. Now with burglaries, a home invasion and stolen property? She couldn't risk leaving the generator outside overnight.

Sam trudged outside and grabbed the handle and started back. She went about a foot and then jerked to an abrupt stop. "What the..." She pointed the flashlight around and noticed a bike chain around the frame with the other end secured around a water spigot. It was a combination one. Ethan must've done it.

Smart kid.

When he was being a smart aleck.

She didn't know the combo and so would have to initiate a conversation sooner than she'd planned. She turned to go back inside and yelped as a figure darted out of the shadows from the side yard. She had just enough time to bring the flashlight up for defense as something swung down at her head.

A metal bat clanged off the flashlight. The blow so hard it bounced the flashlight handle into her head before knocking it out of her grasp. She stumbled backward and the shadow drove her to the ground.

Strong hands closed around her throat.

Her ears rang and her brain buzzed. She grabbed at the sleeves of a black jacket, but couldn't push the arms away. Pressure filled her head and her chest ached for breath.

She clawed at a face deformed by stretched panty hose. The sheer fabric molded the features into a grotesque horror. Her nails came up inches short. The man's arms were longer than hers.

Ethan's voice echoed out of the house. "Mom? Where are you?"

No! She couldn't let him get hurt!

She glanced to the side and saw the flashlight. Grabbed it the instant before her attacker reacted, and then smashed it into his head.

He rocked to the side but somehow managed to keep his fingers locked around her throat. He let go with one hand and snatched the flashlight away.

A smushed, twisted grin opened beneath the

hose. He raised the flashlight over her head. He was too strong. She couldn't stop what would happen next.

A furious growling exploded out the door. Dennis launched into the man, knocking him to the ground. His jaws snapped down on the arm of the jacket.

The man howled with pain.

Sam rolled away as Ethan came outside.

"Mom!"

She spotted the bat and scrambled over to it. She was going to smash this murderer's skull in two. She got to her feet and sucked in a breath to steady herself.

But by then, he had squirmed out of the jacket. He kicked Dennis away and sprinted for the fence.

Dennis gave chase but he vaulted up and over and was gone.

"Come here, boy," Sam said, calling the dog over.

Dennis glanced back, but then returned to a frenzied barking.

Ethan retrieved the flashlight. "Mom, are you okay?" His eyes wide with worry and fear.

She wrapped her arms around him and pulled him close. Tears streamed down her cheeks and slid along the lines of her jaw. "Come on. Let's get inside."

"Are you okay?"

She wasn't crying for her own sake. She would deal with that later. She was crying for her daughter and husband.

If something like this could happen in her own backyard, what horrors might they be facing?

She now realized that she'd gotten lucky. She'd been too slow in coming to terms with this new reality. Things could've easily gone differently and she and her son could've ended up dead.

She'd deal with the guilt later.

Now was the time to get up to speed, and fast.

42

A rooster crowed outside and Cade's eyelids cracked open. He pawed the crust out and saw the pink light of sunrise leaking in around the edges of the curtains. A sick feeling landed in his stomach. A queasy concern that maybe they'd been wrong to trust Wesley. That it was a mistake to have let their guard down and now they were going to pay for it.

He rolled over and saw that the two AR-15 type rifles were leaned against the wall by the side table, exactly where he'd left them the night before. His bags were in a pile on the floor, also exactly where he'd left them.

He let out a big sigh of relief.

Of course they were right where he'd left them.

Wesley wasn't some ridiculously manipulative

villain who gave them a ride for hundreds of miles, fed them a meal fit for a king, gave them a place to sleep, only to then reveal his devious and deadly plan.

Cade pinched his eyes shut, thinking he was an idiot and feeling guilty for doubting someone who was obviously a good person.

By nature, he wasn't a trusting soul. And with the world falling apart like it was, deciding to trust the wrong stranger was enough to get you killed.

Still, it felt like a betrayal to have doubted Wesley even for a second.

A little more awake now, he smelled something in the air that made his stomach grumble with interest. Unless he was very much mistaken, bacon was on the breakfast menu. He swung his legs out to the floor and groaned. Speaking of breakfast favorites, they felt like two bloated sausages.

He had a pretty nice mountain bike back home, but it had been a couple of years since it had gotten regular use. He and Lily used to go out and ride trails just about every week. But that regularity had fallen off the older she got. She'd gotten busier with school and friends and, almost before he knew it, months had gone by without them going out for a ride.

And that was before she got a boyfriend. Before that idiot Colton showed up, acting like a perfect gentleman, doing his best to pull the wool over everyone's eyes.

But Cade had never been fooled. He'd always known the truth. Of course, he hadn't been able to speak that truth. Not with his wife and daughter fawning all over the guy like he could do no wrong.

That all took a one-eighty after Lily dumped his sorry butt. His true colors came out and Cade had been proven right after all. He was still disappointed that Sam had stopped him from beating the snot out of that sniveling punk.

He massaged some feeling into his legs and knew he was going to be hobbling around for a while until the muscles got warmed up. He torqued his chin to the side and got a couple of good cracks out of his neck.

He looked at Hudson sleeping in the bed on the opposite wall of the small room. One of his arms hung off the edge of the twin bed, his hand twitching with whatever was happening in a dream. A trail of drool hung off his lip and connected to the pillow. His head jerked and the tendril jiggled and then broke away, adding to the soaked spot in the cloth.

And that was about all Cade wanted to see of that.

"Time to rise and shine," he said.

No response.

"Sleeping beauty, it's time to get up," he said again, this time at twice the volume.

Still nothing.

He pushed up out of bed and hobbled over. He gave the kid's shoulder a tug and Hudson's eyes blinked open.

They were wide with fear and confusion.

"It's me, Cade. You're okay. Everything's okay."

That wasn't remotely true on the grander scale, but it was true enough for the moment.

Hudson looked around and settled as he remembered where they were. He yanked the covers over his head but that wasn't going to happen.

Cade jerked them back down. "Sleeping time is over. We have to get on the road. Smells like Wesley has breakfast ready."

Hudson cracked one eye open. "Breakfast?"

After a few minutes, they were both up and around. They tidied up the room and headed into the kitchen.

The table had three large bowls with a towel draped over the top of each. A note was next to a couple of plates. In a scrawl that was just this side of intelligible, Wesley told them there was coffee on the stove. And to eat up and that he'd be around.

Cade lifted the towels to reveal scrambled eggs in one bowl, a pile of crispy fried bacon in another, and a half-dozen biscuits in the last. A slab of soft butter and a mason jar of jellied preserves next to that.

Hudson scooped up an empty plate and started piling on the food. "I could get used to this."

"We're not staying. I'm not staying, anyway."

"Are you always like this in the morning?"

"Want some coffee?"

"Does he have a latte machine?"

Cade pointed at the metal kettle on the stove. It was coffee. What more did this kid want?

"Yeah, sure," Hudson said before returning his attention to the growing mound of food on his plate.

Cade poured out a cup for each of them and then filled up a plate of his own. They decided to eat out on the porch and opened the door only to find dozens of eager furry faces staring through the screen door. The whole pack was waiting for them.

"Back it up. Come on, now," Cade said as he eased the screen door open. The pack of insistent beggars fell back enough to let them out, but not an inch more.

They went over to the chairs, but didn't feel comfortable sitting down. Not unless, they were going to hold their plates above their heads while they ate.

A sharp whistle pierced the air.

The beggars turned tail and ran. They spilled down the steps like a dam broke loose.

Wesley waved on his way over from the barn. "Morning! Hope my mongrels didn't clean you out."

"Good morning," Cade said as he took a seat. "No, they're fine. And thank you for this. For all of this."

Hudson held up a slice of bacon. "Is this organic?"

Cade pinched his eyes shut. There was a time and place, and this wasn't it. He wondered if the kid would ever clue in to that.

Wesley pulled off a pair of dusty work gloves as he came up the stairs. "You not going to eat it if it isn't?"

Hudson folded the long strip into his mouth in answer.

Wesley chuckled. "I suppose you all will be off today."

Cade murmured affirmation through a mouth full of eggs.

"I wanted to talk to you about that. There may be a better way for you to get to Vegas than hopping back on those bikes."

That got Cade's attention.

Which was really saying something because the flaky, buttery biscuit layered with a dollop of strawberry preserves was all he could think about one second before.

43

Cade returned the biscuit to his plate. "What did you have in mind?"

Wesley ran a hand over his damp, white hair. The sun was barely above the horizon and he'd clearly been hard at work for hours. He scooped up Queen Lottie out of the middle of the pack, passed around a few scratches to the others and then joined them on the porch.

"I have a friend, well, not a friend. I know a guy who is a bit of a tinkerer with all things mechanical. Cars especially. He never met a wreck he didn't like. He brings some of them back from the dead, but mostly I think he just likes collecting."

He poured himself a glass of water from the

pitcher on the railing and gulped it down. He filled it up again and let Lottie lap out of the glass.

She was definitely queen of the castle. And the rest of the pack gathered round the bottom step appeared to be okay with that. Maybe they knew she needed the extra attention.

"You think he would sell us one? I've got cash." Cade thought of the money in his belt and also the money he'd scavenged off a few corpses.

Wesley shook his head. "Nah, I don't think so. He doesn't have much use for paper money. He operates more in a barter economy. You'd have to trade him something."

Cade went through a mental inventory of their few possessions. They didn't have much.

"I don't want to put words into his mouth, but I bet he'd trade one of his working wrecks for one of those rifles you picked up yesterday."

The two AR-15s.

With a long journey ahead, scoring them had been an unexpected windfall. The extra firepower could end up being the difference between making it and not. Then again, they still had a long way to go to Vegas, let alone Durango. And he was not looking forward to getting back on the bike. His sit bones ached like he'd had a run in with a bucking bull.

Could he part with one?

It wouldn't be like he'd be defenseless without it.

"I could do that," Cade said, wiping some jelly from his chin. "For the right car."

"Well, I'll take you over when you're finished with breakfast."

"You don't have to do that," Cade said.

Wesley waved him off. "I've been meaning to go by anyway. He's had a busted irrigation pump of mine forever and might need a kick in the pants to remember that I want it fixed."

They plowed through the rest of their plates and helped clean up inside. After putting their things in the back of the farm truck, they pulled away and Cade watched the quaint little farmhouse slide by.

The yapping, howling, barking pack followed at first, but fell away by the time they made it to the main road and pulled up onto the pavement.

"Thanks again for putting us up for the night," Cade said.

"Seriously, I almost feel human," Hudson added.

Cade thought he saw the flash of a smile on the kid's face. That was good.

"It was my pleasure. I don't get many visitors and it's nice to talk with someone who walks on two legs for a change."

"Have you always lived alone?" Hudson asked.

A sadness creased the lines in Wesley's face. "No. I was married for forty-one years to the one and only love of my life. Mrs. Mabel Guthrie. We couldn't have children but there were always folks around back then. The Lord took her thirteen years ago. Went to the doctor about some dizzy spells that wouldn't go away. Found out it was cancer in her brain. It didn't take long from there."

He swallowed hard and cleared his throat. A gruff laugh came out. "She never would've allowed the farm to be taken over by those mongrels, I'll tell you what. She was a good woman, but she was particular."

He seemed to drift into memories.

Out of the corner of his eye, Cade saw that Hudson had done the same.

They rode the rest of the way in quiet contemplation, until they pulled up to a tall chain link gate with barbed wire coiled along the top. It connected to a span of similar fencing that stretched out to the sides and wrapped around a large property.

A piece of plywood strapped to the gate had a warning in red spray paint.

TRESPASSERS WILL BE SHOT AND FED TO THE DOGS!

The inside of the fence was filled with dilapidated wrecks. Some missing hoods, trunks, fenders, doors. One a bare chassis with wheels but no tires. A relatively newer one had a puddle of oil underneath. Nature had taken over the rusted out older ones. Weeds grew out the windows and through the engine blocks.

Three Doberman Pinchers hopped out of open trunks and charged over to the fence, barking their heads off and showing their teeth. The message was loud and clear. Step a foot inside and they would tear it clean off.

Two ramshackle mobile homes sat back a ways from the fence. Plastic tarps draped over the roofs were held down by car tires. The siding was peeling away and had been replaced by a mishmash of random materials where it wasn't. It looked like it had been repaired with whatever happened to be closest. Black polysheet, plywood, corrugated metal, a shed door. A wood pallet was stacked with five gallon propane tanks.

There was more, but that was more than enough to cause concern.

"How well do you know this guy?" Cade asked.

"I know him. Like I said, we're not friends

because I'd never choose to spend time with him beyond doing business."

"Why is that?"

"You'll see," Wesley said as he climbed out of the truck and approached the fence.

The dogs went rabid in response.

Wesley stopped a couple of feet short and yelled. "Eugene! You in there?"

He yelled a few more times, but eventually gave up. He returned to the truck and laid on the horn until one of the trailer doors flew open.

A man came out swearing up a storm carrying a shotgun under his arm. No shirt and overalls with only one shoulder holding them up. Bare feet crusted in dirt. A silver flame of hair sticking up on top. He yelled at the dogs to shut up as he moseyed over. He stopped a few feet away from the gate, but made no move to open it.

"Who are you and what do you want?"

Wesley met him outside. "Can you just let us in already?"

The old man shot a stink eye at Cade and Hudson still sitting in the truck. "You, maybe. Them, no."

Wesley blew out an exasperated breath. "They're looking for a working vehicle."

Eugene shrugged. "So. What's that got to do with me?"

"They're willing to trade for it."

Eugene's gray eyes sparkled with life, but then he got suspicious again. "Who are they?"

"Friends of mine."

"How come I ain't never seen these so-called friends of yours around here?"

"They're new friends."

"So you don't really know them then, do you?"

"For crying out loud, Eugene. Open the stupid gate!"

He considered a minute and then nodded. "Let me put the pups away. Wouldn't want anyone losing a hand."

If those were the kind of pups that popped out of boxes at Christmas, kids everywhere would be dying of shock.

Eugene returned a few minutes later and let them in. As soon as the truck was inside, he slammed the gate shut and secured the chain and padlock.

Cade and Hudson climbed out and Wesley circled around to make the introductions. He got a few words into it, but Eugene cut him off.

"So you're looking to trade, huh?"

Cade nodded.

He spat a glob of tobacco juice into the dirt, close but not onto Cade's boot.

So the negotiations had already begun.

"That is assuming any of these junkers are worth anything." Cade nodded toward a rusted out heap with a missing roof that had sunflowers growing up where the front seat should've been. "I'm looking for something that drives, something reliable. Not a flowerpot."

Eugene's eyes narrowed. "Let's step into my office to discuss it."

44

Cade didn't budge. "No sense discussing anything if all you have is what I see around here."

Eugene stuttered to a stop.

Wesley's brow arched and he fought to keep from snickering.

"All this up here is for the lookie loo's driving by. The good stuff is in the back." He pivoted in that direction and started walking.

"Does that mean we're supposed to follow?" Hudson whispered.

Cade waved him on and followed.

Eugene took them on a tour through a couple of large outbuildings, showing and talking up various resurrected wrecks.

Cade rejected one after the other with a single

glance, until they came to an old rusted black GMC truck.

Eugene fired it up and the engine sounded decent enough.

Cade looked under the hood and didn't see anything obviously wrong. He wasn't a mechanic per se, but he'd gotten his hands covered in grease often enough. Usually from replacing a part on his wife's Volvo. The truck looked like a winner, but he wasn't about to say that. "Lot of wear and tear here. I'd be surprised if it makes it a hundred miles before going croak."

Eugene scowled. "It may not look it, but this one is as solid as they come. We'll die before it finally goes to the junkyard in the sky."

They went back and forth a couple of minutes. Cade pointing out every flaw he could find while Eugene lavished praise on it like there'd never been a better vehicle ever built.

Cade turned the conversation to the terms of the trade but Eugene wouldn't discuss it further until they retired to his office.

Calling it an office turned out to be quite an exaggeration. Like calling a Ford Pinto a luxury mode of transportation. Or calling a stick of Slim Jim beef jerky a t-bone steak. Yeah, they were technically both from cows, but that was where the likeness ended.

The trashed out interior of Eugene's trailer was an office only in so far as he was eventually able to sweep away enough debris so that they all had a place to sit.

Except for Hudson.

He chose to remain standing.

Cade would've done the same if it wouldn't have interfered with the negotiations. As it was, he and Eugene sat across a filthy table and volleyed offers and counteroffers back and forth. Knowing the game, he'd started off by offering low, but not too low.

Hudson's bike.

That got a frown from the kid, but he was smart enough to chip in with details about what made it elite and so valuable.

That the negotiations went on a while didn't surprise Cade in the least. This was probably the most fun Eugene had had in weeks.

Cade eventually allowed himself to be cornered into giving up one of the AR-15s along with an extra magazine. But he managed to secure a full tank of gas on top of the truck itself.

The deal concluded and Eugene beamed with

satisfaction. Partly because Cade made sure to act sour and unhappy about the whole thing.

"This deserves a drink!" Eugene said. He rummaged through a pile of dishes in the sink and dug out a couple of shot glasses. He slapped them on the table and scooped up a mason jar of clear liquid.

Cade stared at the streaked glass with disgust. He didn't want to scuttle the deal by refusing to drink. Besides, whatever was in that jar was definitely going to be strong enough to kill any bacteria.

Eugene was in the process of spilling liquid into both glasses when someone yelled outside.

That sent the dogs into a barking frenzy from wherever they were being kept.

Eugene cursed and took a look through the blinds. He cursed again and set the jar on the table. "Everybody's coming by today, huh?" He grabbed up the newly acquired AR-15 and kicked the door open on the way out.

Cade pulled the blinds over and saw a group of five guys outside the fence. All armed but not behaving in a threatening way. Still, he didn't like the looks of them. They had a bad vibe.

Wesley glanced out the window and muttered something.

"Who are they?"

"The Puckett brothers. All tweakers. Methheads from the next town over. I told that idiot not to get involved with them."

With the dogs barking, it was impossible to hear the conversation happening at the fence. Whatever was being said finally came to an end. And it didn't look like there were any bad feelings.

Eugene turned around and started back to the trailer.

And then one of the Puckett brothers raised a pistol and shot him in the back. And kept shooting until he ran out of bullets.

"We have to go!" Cade said when one of them pulled out bolt cutters and got to work on the chain. Going out the door wasn't an option. He didn't want to fire on them either because the trailer would've been no cover at all. Like hiding behind a slice of cheese.

He hurried to the back bedroom and almost tumbled forward when the floor gave way underfoot. He tested the squishy part and saw it was barely holding together. He stomped on it to finish the job and kept going until the hole was big enough to get through.

The voices outside grew louder. They were inside the fence and heading toward the trailer.

Cade helped Wesley down, then Hudson and then dropped through himself.

The trailer door slammed open as they crawled out the back side. Fortunately, the barking dogs covered the sounds of their escape. They stayed low and ran toward the back of the property. They skirted along the fence until they came upon a hole dug underneath. The dogs must've dug it out and Eugene hadn't noticed or didn't care.

They squeezed under the fence, the sharp ends of the cut wires snagging and tearing at their clothes as they went.

Cade was the last one out and all three hurried into the adjacent woods. They went in far enough to be sure they wouldn't be seen.

Wesley was shaking his head. "How many times did I tell him?"

It wasn't a question he was expecting an answer for.

"Why did they shoot him?" Hudson asked.

Wesley shrugged. "I don't know. Maybe a drug deal gone bad? I never knew Eugene to be into drugs though. Moonshine and tobacco and the occasional joint were all I've ever seen. But I never claimed to know all his doings."

"They have all of our stuff," Hudson said.

And that was exactly what Cade had been chewing on. With the bikes and all their belongings in the back of Wesley's truck, they had next to nothing. He had his handgun and that was it.

"What are we going to do?" Hudson asked.

"We're going to get back what is rightfully ours," Cade said.

Walking away wasn't an option. But taking on five armed and proven killers wasn't a great option either.

Cade leaned against a tree and took a seat. "Might as well take a load off. We're going to be here a while. When night falls, we'll sneak back and see what our options are. Who knows? Maybe we'll get lucky and they'll leave."

As much as it burned him to have to waste the daylight not getting closer to his daughter, he also knew that not getting to her at all would be far worse.

45

With the windows down and the warm evening air blowing in, Donny should've been in a better mood. He would've been if his idiot friend and supposed business partner Zeke hadn't lost the directions to Jax's place. Without Google Maps, it wasn't like they could just punch in the address and follow the directions.

They'd been driving around for the last hour and he was about to lose it. What if they never found it? No one missed an appointment with Jax. No one that wanted to live, anyway. And especially no one that already owed him money.

A stray dog appeared in the road and Donny hit the gas and aimed the Mino at it. The dog darted to safety at the last second and Donny cursed out the window as they roared by.

Stupid strays. They infested parts of Vegas like fleas. The Mino's bumper had a few dings on it that proved he didn't always miss.

Donny slammed on the brakes in the middle of a two lane on the western edge of the city. "When was the last time you for sure saw the paper with the directions?"

"I told you a thousand times, man. It was in my jacket. I remember seeing it this afternoon."

"Then how did it disappear? Is it magic paper? Now it's there, now it's not?"

Zeke snarled and looked away out the passenger window.

Muffled sounds came from the bed of the Mino. Sugar and Spice were tied up together with a tarp strapped over the top.

Donny pounded on the back of the cab. "Shut up!"

The noise quieted.

He'd initially been worried about running across the cops, but that had turned out to be no problem at all. They hadn't come across a single cop the whole way. They'd passed a number of cop cars, but those were broke and abandoned like every other vehicle on the road.

Just about every other vehicle, anyway.

There had been a couple of cars driving around, but they'd taken off like a shot the second the Mino came into view. That was when Donny started to realize that the Mino was worth more than he was thinking. Sure, it had more dents and dings and scratches than a soda can in a tornado, but it worked.

And for some reason, all those nicer, newer cars were dead as door nails.

It was something to keep in mind.

Something had happened the other night. Something big. Maybe it was some kind of alien technology thing out in Area 51. Maybe the government tried to use some ET weapon and it blew up in their faces.

Donny figured things would go back to normal before too long. Which was why it was so important to take advantage while they could. This was a window of opportunity and they had to grab hold with both hands while the grabbing was good.

And that meant getting to Jax's or else Zeke didn't have to worry about Jax taking him out. Donny would.

No joke.

If stepping into his bigger and better future meant stepping on a part of his old, pathetic life... well, so be it.

"Check your pockets again!" Donny said, not trying in the least to keep calm about it. He flipped on the overhead light and gripped the steering wheel like it was a neck that needed strangling. He glanced in the rear view window and liked what he saw. The leather motorcycle jacket he'd found at the Mandalay made him look like a real badass. At least he'd gotten something out of that deal.

Zeke sighed. "I've already checked them fifty times today. I don't have it."

Donny smacked the wheel in frustration. He glared at Zeke and was considering punching him in the jaw when he noticed something. A vertical slit in the side of Zeke's pants. He reached over and discovered it was a pocket. "Did you check there?"

Zeke looked down in confusion. "What?"

"That's a pocket, isn't it?"

Zeke's eyes went wide. He dug his fingers in and pulled out a folded piece of paper. His pale cheeks blushed pink. "I forgot... I didn't... sorry... I put..."

Donny snatched it away and barely managed to resist the urge to backhand him for being such an idiot. His best and only friend in the world might not be cut out for anything more than being a druggie loser. It could be an unavoidable truth. He'd have to think more about it later. If it was time to cut him loose, better to do it now. The bigger the business, the more costly mistakes became. He couldn't and wouldn't allow Zeke to drag him down. He filed it away for now and read through the directions.

It took a while to get back on track, but he managed and before long they found Jax's place. Place was the understatement of the century.

It was a compound surrounded by ten foot high solid walls with sharp, decorative spikes lining the top. The driveway led to a rolling gate with an adjacent guardhouse. The gate wasn't the usual black wrought iron bars that they'd seen at other large properties along the way. No, this one was solid metal panels welded onto thick beams. And whereas the others had snooty names like Rising Moon Ranch or Majestic Foothills Ranch (both in gold cursive letters), this one had no name and didn't look the least bit inviting.

A bulky guard wearing a dark suit and tie came out of the guardhouse with his hand up for them to stop. And if that hand didn't get the message across, the Uzi submachine-gun in the other definitely did.

It wasn't pointed at them, but half a second could change that. He came over to the window and looked them over. "You're late."

Donny chuckled and hooked a thumb at Zeke. "My friend here lost the instructions."

Zeke gave a thin smile. "I did, but I found them."

The guard gave them both a hard stare. He didn't appear to be big on humor.

"Mr. Cook was expecting you to bring merchandise."

"They're under the tarp in the back," Donny said.

"Both of you get out," he said.

"What?" Donny said.

The muzzle of the gun shifted over to them. "Get out. Now."

Donny threw his hands up. "Whoa! Easy there. You don't want to kill Jax's new cash cows." He opened the door and stepped out. Zeke came around to join them.

The guard patted them both down and then rifled through the Mino's interior. He found the revolver under Donny's seat and brought it out looking very unhappy.

"Hey, I would've told you about it but you didn't ask."

The guard wasn't convinced. "No weapons are

allowed inside the property until Mr. Cook personally says otherwise. Nothing on your person or in your vehicle. Is there anything else that needs to be left with me?"

Donny shook his head. "Nope. That's it." And he wasn't lying because he had no intention of turning over the .22 handgun tucked into the secret spot under the dash. It was small enough to fit there and would be better than nothing if he ended up needing it.

"Show me what's in the back," he said.

"No problem," Donny said. "But could you point that somewhere else? We're on the same side here."

The guard did as instructed.

Donny winked and smiled with satisfaction. This was how it was supposed to be. Him giving the orders and other people doing as they were told. Maybe he'd let this bonehead work for him after he took over Jax's business and became the big boss. He untied the tarp and revealed the girls underneath. They were tightly bound back to back and then strapped down to anchor latches in the corners of the bed.

The guard nodded. "Take the driveway to the main house. Security will be there to escort you inside."

Donny's heart leaped in his chest. His fingertips tingled with possibility. Most days didn't matter. They passed by in a blur of meaningless moments. But this one was different.

This was the first day of the rest of his life.

This was where all the tragedy and failure and disappointment ended.

46

The tarp flew off and Donny flashed an evil grin at Lily. She'd come to understand him to a degree over the last day and a half. He was a methhead, yes. But that wasn't it. He was also a psychopath. She and Piper weren't human beings to him. They were pieces in his sick game. Things that were only cared for in so far as that care served his purpose.

She knew he'd only given them food and water because it served his purpose. The fact that they were hungry and thirsty hadn't ever been a factor in it.

Donny vaulted into the back and untied them enough to drag them out. He left their wrists bound behind their backs and the gags over their mouths.

He passed them off to a couple of guards standing by the vehicle.

Lily groaned as the feeling of pins and needles spread through her numbed limbs. She would've collapsed but thick arms held her upright.

Piper had gone silent earlier that day. It was like she'd finally run out of tears. Dark mascara streaked her cheeks. Her empty eyes stared at nothing. Lily hadn't been able to get her to say a word in hours.

She wasn't sure why that mattered. Maybe Piper's approach was better. Go numb and stay that way. She'd done it herself the night before. After failing in the attempt to escape. After Donny had kicked her and put his hands on her.

All she'd wanted to do was vanish.

And she had, for a time.

But she couldn't stay gone.

Something inside her refused to. Something inside her wouldn't surrender. It wanted to fight. It wanted revenge. It wanted to claw Donny's eyes out and kick out his remaining teeth.

The anger gave her strength. But strength for what?

All of her struggle had only earned her worse treatment. She'd fought again and again, and it had resulted in nothing but bruises. Piper's surrender had earned her gentler treatment.

Not that it mattered now.

Several black SUVs were parked around the circular cobblestone driveway. A fountain with statues of galloping horses occupied the space in the center. Water kicked up around their hooves like dust. Lights shone on their sides, accentuating the ripple of muscle and tendon. A generator hummed from somewhere in the distance.

The house itself was a sprawling single-story structure of white stucco with a roof of layered terracotta tiles. Black iron bars covered the multitude of windows. Most were dark, but several glowed with soft light.

"Mr. Cook is waiting inside," one of the guards said. All three wore dark suits with slicked back hair. All tall and huge. Their unnatural bulk suggested they'd never met a steroid they didn't like. Each had an Uzi submachine-gun hanging off a shoulder.

Donny plucked at the collar of his leather jacket. "Let's not keep the boss waiting then."

The guard carried as much as walked Lily up the stairs to a grand arched entrance with polished wood double doors. They went inside and threaded through a maze of rooms and corridors until they arrived at the back patio. Only, this wasn't a back patio like Lily had ever seen. Not in real life, anyway.

An outdoor living room with couches, chairs and everything. A low glass table in the middle. A stone fireplace on one end with a roaring fire inside. An outdoor kitchen next to that with stainless steel appliances and colorful mosaic tile countertops. A huge grill with the top open and slabs of meat sizzling inside. Beyond that, a pool that stretched the width of both spaces. A mound of irregular rock along the back and a yawning darkness where the pool went into a cave underneath. Off to the side, a pool house so big that it wouldn't have looked out of place in any normal neighborhood in Durango.

A pair of guards strolled by and disappeared on the path behind the pool house. Others stood at what must've been their assigned posts because they didn't move much, just kept looking around.

One of the doors to the pool house opened and a man in a black silk robe strolled out. He pulled the cigar out of his mouth and blew out a cloud of gray smoke. He saw them and raised his arms in welcome. The robe parted revealing a protruding beer belly, black silk boxers and legs as thick as tree trunks. "Our guests have finally arrived. I was beginning to worry about you." The cold look in his eyes made clear the meaning.

"We're so sorry for—" Donny said as he started forward.

A huge paw of a hand clamped down on his shoulder to keep him in place.

"Jax," Donny winced, making it clear the guard wasn't being gentle. "Mr. Cook, I mean. We're sorry for being late. We got a little lost on the way out here. No Google Maps is like living in the stone ages, you know?"

Jax stopped in front of Donny and looked up at him.

Lily didn't know what she was expecting, but it was taller than this.

Even with the difference in height, it was Donny that shrank away.

Jax let the tension simmer as he glowered. His expression finally softened and he smiled. "Don't let it happen again."

"We won't," Zeke chimed in.

Jax cast a glance his way. "Donny, you're lucky to have such a good friend here. If it wasn't for him, you'd be dead right now."

Donny laughed nervously. "Yep, we go way back. Always been there for each other. Always will."

Jax turned to Lily and slowly ran his eyes up the length of her until their eyes met.

She wanted to look away. There was a cold cruelty in his gaze that made the hairs on the back of her neck prickle.

He took a lock of her hair.

She jerked her head away but he held tight with a clump in his fist. He brushed out some matted dirt. "What happened to this one?"

"That's Spice," Donny said. "I had to be rough a couple times to settle her down. Nothing that caused permanent damage. She's fine. But she'll need some breaking in."

Jax's lips spread into a smirk.

Lily's stomach twisted with fear and disgust. A part of her wanted to scream and fight. Another part had already given up.

Jax sidestepped to Piper. He laid a hand on her hip and she flinched but didn't pull away. He ran it down and squeezed her butt. "And this one?"

"That's Sugar. Doesn't have the same spirit, but look at that body. You know she'll be good where it counts."

Jax nodded. He gestured toward the living area. "Come, we have business to discuss."

His eyes lingered on Lily an instant. He smiled.

And she'd never felt so cold. So drowned with overwhelming dread.

Donny slapped her butt as he sauntered by. "You be a good girl, Spice. Or not. He'll break you either way." He winked and walked away.

47

Lily and Piper had been alone for a couple of hours and barely a word had passed between them. Piper still wasn't talking. They were seated on the cement floor, each with their backs against a thick pole that was bolted to the floor and ceiling. She would've called it a stripper pole, but now it had more ominous uses. It was for enslaving girls. For keeping them prisoner.

A guard had taken them to the room inside the house while Jax and Donny concluded their dirty business. Two hours had passed and the growing volume of noise beyond the door suggested it had turned into a party, and they were getting more and more messed up.

Lily had tried to get free for the first hour or so,

but had only succeeded in grinding up the skin on her wrists. She'd never felt so helpless. She'd always believed she could do anything. Been told that by her parents for as long as she could remember. And sure, she'd failed along the way like anyone, but she'd succeeded more. And she always knew that if it came down to it, she could deliver no matter the odds.

But she'd never faced anything like this.

She'd never lived in a world like this one.

"Piper," she said, hoping to get any kind of response from her friend.

Piper's head hung down, her chin on her chest. Her knit dress filthy and torn in places. The bandages on her knees had come off and the wounds needed attention. The mismatched sneakers added to her tragic appearance.

Lily wanted to help, but she couldn't. She could barely move and besides, her backpack was on the kitchen counter in the squatter's house. She couldn't help her physically, but the physical injuries weren't the worst problem.

"Piper, talk to me. Please. I'm worried about you."

Piper's head slowly turned. "Me?"

"Yeah."

"Why not you? You're trapped here too."

"I know. But we're going to get out."

Piper's eyes closed and her head slumped down again. "There is no way out. And we both know what's going to happen next."

Lily swallowed hard. She had an idea and she'd been struggling not to think about it the whole time. Letting her mind go there wouldn't do anything good. It would drag her down into despair as it had to Piper. And she couldn't let that happen.

She had to be aware and ready. If she gave up, they were both done.

The lock clicked and the door opened.

A guard came in and cut the ties away from Lily's wrists.

She yanked one hand free and swung at him but he caught her by the elbow and squeezed. Pain shot through her arm, driving the breath out of her lungs.

"Don't be stupid," he grumbled.

"Let go of me!" she screamed.

He wrenched her arms behind her back and held the wrists together with a single, giant vise-like hand. He wrapped a thick arm around her chest and picked her up like she weighed nothing.

"Let go of me!" Lily said.

He turned and headed for the door.

She glanced over her shoulder and saw Piper's

sad eyes before the door swung shut. She kicked up behind her, hoping to connect with his groin but he was too fast.

He squeezed on her wrists and sharp pain exploded. She gasped and tears welled in her eyes.

"Warned you."

She wanted to fight, but the shock had numbed her arms.

The guard carried her through the house and finally down a long hall. He stopped at the door and knocked.

"Come," a voice said.

They entered a large bedroom with French doors on the far wall that opened onto the back patio. Several lamps spilled pools of light throughout the room. A four poster bed with thick carved pillars of dark wood at each corner with connecting spans at the top. A long dresser of the same material hugged one wall. A doorway opened to a bathroom filled with white marble.

Jax strolled out of the bathroom with his robe open and a drink in hand. "Ahh, the reason for the party." He pointed at a bedpost.

The guard dragged her over and zip tied her wrists around it. "Need anything, boss?"

Jax waved him away and he left. "Spice, huh?" he

said as he did something with a silver tray on top of the dresser. He leaned down and snorted up what Lily realized must've been a huge line of coke. He spun around, sniffing and pinching at his nostrils. White dust clung to his upper lip. "Whoa!" he said and snapped his head to the side. "That'll put some giddy up in your saddle!"

He knocked back a few gulps of something amber-colored and set the glass down. Only he set it on the edge of the dresser. It fell to the floor and shattered. "Dammit!" He swept his sandal across the shards, pushing them under the dresser. "You can clean that up later." He held out the silver tray to her. A pile of coke, razor blades and short straws were on top. "Want some?"

Lily glared at him.

He shrugged. "You will, eventually. They all do." He set the tray down and came over to her. Bits of coke clung to his scruffy upper lip. He put a hand on her knee and she tried to pull away, but his grip was immovable. Even stronger than the guard's who'd brought her in here. He grabbed her other knee and pushed her legs apart. He stepped forward and his round belly pressed against her.

She turned her head away. He was a vile, repugnant beast and the heavy splash of cologne did little to mask the animal odor underneath.

"What's your name?"

"My dad will find you and he'll kill you when he does."

Jax let out a boisterous laugh. "Donny was right! You are a wild one. Do you want to know a little secret?"

She didn't answer. She was sure he had a million secrets, all of them horrible.

"No? I'll tell you anyway." He grabbed her jaws, smashing her mouth from the sides, and wrenched her head forward. "I'm a wealthy man and have the means to own many horses. I've broken every last one myself. Do you know why?"

"Because you're a sick bastard?" Lily's eyes flared with hatred.

"Because breaking their will gets me hard. I enjoy the battle as much as that final moment of triumph. The more challenging the horse, the more exciting the fight and the sweeter the moment of inevitable capitulation."

"So you're a horse pervert?" Lily didn't get long to enjoy that because he clamped down on her jaws. The pressure made the bones creak.

His eyes froze over. "I'm going to break you. It

will hurt and it will leave scars. But, in the end, you'll be begging for more."

She spat in his face. It was all she could do.

He backhanded her across the face.

Her head snapped to the side and blood rushed through her neck, nearly making her pass out.

He stepped away, wiping at his face. "Okay. So you need to be muzzled. I've got just this thing." He walked into a large closet. Drawers opened and closed.

Lily slipped down off the bed with her wrists still bound around the bedpost. She kicked her feet out to the dresser, and to the shards of glass underneath. She strained one foot out as far as it would go.

The toe touched a jagged fragment. She nudged it across the tile floor and carefully gripped it between her shoes. She rolled back on the bed and doubled over to get the shard into her hands.

She palmed it as a drawer in the closet slammed shut and then Jax reappeared.

He stopped when he saw her. "You're not going to break that post. And those zip ties will cut you to the bone before they fail."

With one hand hiding the other, she was already sawing away at one of them.

He came over and dangled something in front of

her face. He forced her mouth open and shoved the ball inside. He secured the straps behind her neck and head. He pulled a knife out of his robe and flicked it open.

The five-inch blade glinted in the lamp light.

Lily's heart ran like a rabbit in her chest. So fast she was getting dizzy. Her breaths came in shallow pants.

"You might want to hold still," he said with a leer. He grabbed her shirt by the collar and sliced it open down the front. He hooked the tip under the center of her bra. A flick slashed it apart and exposed her breasts.

She cut through the last zip tie and her hands came free. She punched the fragment straight into his eye.

He screamed and dropped the knife. He clutched at the glass embedded in his eye socket. Blood poured down his cheek.

Lily froze for an instant, terrified that guards would hear and come bursting through the door. But they were being so loud, and probably so drunk, that none heard.

Lily snatched up the knife and sawed away the restraints around her ankles. She bounced off the bed and started for the door, but a hand clamped around her upper arm and hauled her backward.

Jax hurled her onto the bed. He reached for her neck, but she batted the hand away.

She slammed the knife to the side and it drove through his palm and deep into the bedpost.

He shrieked in agony, his free hand caught in the middle between the ruin of his eye and the hand pinned to the dark wood.

Lily yanked the knife out, rolled away and didn't look back.

She had to get Piper and get out.

Before it was too late.

48

Lily tied her shirt together and ran down the hall. She ducked behind a corner when voices drew near.

A couple of guards walked by. Beer bottles in hand. One telling a story about a boosted car while the other laughed and toasted the life of crime. Both with dusty white haloes around their nostrils.

She waited until they passed and then took off again. Mind racing faster than her feet, she traced the way back to where Piper was being held and tried the door.

Locked.

"Piper!" she said through the door. "Piper, are you in there?"

"Lily?" a scared voice replied.

She was there! Not taken into some other room and forced to endure what Lily had escaped.

"Yes!" She stepped back and then lunged into a kick below the handle. The door shook but held. She tried again and this time it burst open. Splinters of wood bounced across the floor.

She dropped next to Piper and cut away the zip ties. Adrenaline surged through her veins, making her hands tremble. A cut went too far and the knife cut into Piper's skin.

"Oww!"

"Sorry!" Lily got through the remaining restraints. She pulled Piper to her feet. "We're leaving."

Piper nodded, her face a mix of fear and hope.

Lily led the way out and down the hall. They were almost to the front entrance when voices approached from that direction.

"I want her found! Now! And get the other one!"

Jax. And between groans, he was livid.

Lily cut around a corner and hurried through an expansive living room and then through a library, a study and the kitchen. She peered through the windows and didn't see anyone on the back patio. All the guards must've been looking for them. "Come on!"

They raced outside and the plan was to... she didn't have a plan. Not a complicated one, anyway.

The plan was to get away as fast as possible.

They looped around the pool and she was about to lead them down the path to the rear of the property when voices came from that direction. She spun around and saw dark silhouettes moving in the kitchen.

"In here," she hissed as she dragged Piper into the pool house. It was a large room with a bar on one side. Beer and liquor bottles covered the counter. Ash trays with piles of stubbed out cigarettes. One had a cigarette with the end still burning, a tendril of smoke curling up to the ceiling.

Shuffling sounds came from the doorway on the other side of the room. She turned and pushed through a closed door.

And ended up in a bathroom.

The toilet flushed and someone stepped out of the stall.

Donny.

He stared in confusion for a second, and then spotted the knife in her hand. He reached behind his back, but Lily was already on him.

She drove the knife at his chest but he managed to dodge to the side and they both crashed down in a jumbled heap. The fall knocked the knife out of her hand.

But it was there, within reach.

She grabbed at it, but then his fist hammered into her head, knocking her to the side. Her head hit the floor with a sickening crunch. She tried to sit up and warmth spread down her neck.

Donny shoved her back down and straddled her chest, pinning her arms under his legs. The knife appeared in his hand. He twisted it above her face. "I'm going to cut you up, Spice. Make you wish you were dead." The cruel grin on his face made it clear he wanted nothing more.

She stopped fighting and relaxed all her muscles at once. Went completely limp. The abrupt change caught him off guard.

And that was all she needed.

Lily bucked upward with all of her strength. If he'd been sitting on her stomach or lower, it wouldn't have worked. But on her chest it did.

She flung him forward and then turned around and jumped on his back. She found the handgun tucked into his waistband, got it, and fired.

Two shots in the back.

It was better than the bastard deserved.

A voice outside.

An idea hit Lily in a flash. She dug into Donny's jacket pockets and found the car keys.

The bathroom door opened and Zeke walked in.

Lily turned the gun on him, ready to take him down too.

"What did you do? What did you do?" Zeke ignored her and collapsed next to Donny. He rolled him onto his side. "Hey, buddy. Come on, now." Tears streamed down his cheeks and his words slipped into blubbering incoherence.

Lily guided Piper out the door and they snuck outside. Shouting voices echoed around, but no one was on the back patio. They slipped around the side of the house.

The sound of someone running and they ducked into some bushes. The runner passed and they continued on. After avoiding another close call, they got to the front and jumped into Donny's car. The Mino, as he called it. It was actually a slave wagon, but it was their way out.

Lily cranked on the ignition. "Put on your seatbelt!" She hit the gas and nearly crashed straight into one of the SUVs. She managed to broadside it and keep going. She hit the pedal as they drove away. A glance in the rearview mirror showed Jax standing in the driveway, cradling his injured eye. A bandage already around the injured hand. He yelled something, but she couldn't hear over the roar of the engine.

The tires squealed around a curve and the gate came into view. "Hold on!" Lily yelled as she fastened her own seat belt.

They hit the gate like a thunderclap.

The seatbelt bit into her hips and across her chest.

The gate bent and bounced to the side, and they were through!

She cranked the wheel over and the end fishtailed out to the side. The car spun around in a full three-sixty before lurching to a stop.

Bullets pounded into the side of the car. One hit the rear glass and it shattered.

She gripped the steering wheel with both hands and stomped down on the accelerator.

Another spray of bullets thunked into the car, but they were off!

The headlights were destroyed and it was dangerously dark even with the moonlight. She nearly drove them into a ditch at the end of the road.

They screeched to a stop with the front tires on the last inch of pavement.

She backed up and turned onto a new road. The

city spread out before them in the distance. Glints of moonlight shone on the windows of the tallest buildings. That had to be the strip. The Mandalay was south of those buildings.

Lily oriented herself to the map in her head and drove on. She reached across the seat, found Piper's hand and squeezed. "We're going to be okay."

"Are you sure?"

"Yes, I am."

She wasn't. But Piper needed reassurance, not Vegas style odds on whether they were going to survive or not. They'd gotten away from Donny, Zeke, and Jax.

That was enough for now.

49

Night fell and Cade's grand plan to wait until they had the advantage of darkness wasn't quite turning out like he'd hoped. The sounds coming from inside the fence were not encouraging. More and more voices filled the air. It was turning into a huge party. The increasingly drunken shouting and crack of shots fired as the evening turned into night scuttled the first twenty plans they'd bandied back and forth during the long wait.

There wasn't going to be any sneaking in and driving Wesley's truck away before anyone was the wiser. If anything, it sounded like there was ten times as many people now, and more importantly, ten times as many guns.

It sounded like the Fourth of July in there. Yet another burst of gunfire followed by a round of raucous shouting and inebriated laughter.

No, this wasn't getting any easier.

Cade stood up and paced back and forth, but pacing wasn't getting them closer to recovering their belongings either. He cursed under his breath and decided he'd had enough. "I'm going to go take a look."

He crept through the forest, headed back to the fence perimeter, until he heard the snap of branches and swishing of leaves on his heels. He turned and Hudson nearly bumped into him. "What are you doing?"

"I'm coming with you. To help."

Cade pinched his eyes shut. "Do you have a weapon?"

"No."

"Do you have a plan for how exactly one of us with a handgun can take out what sounds like fifty or more armed idiots?"

"No."

"Then get the hell back there and wait until I return."

"No."

"What?"

"I want to help."

Cade ran a hand over his face. "Tell you what. You can help by staying right here and being ready for when I come back with news about what I've seen. It'll be your job to make sure everything is okay right here. Got it?"

Hudson's eyes lit up. He was now an important part of the plan and he was committed to doing his best. "I'll be right here. You can count on me."

Cade fought off an exasperated sigh and even said "Sounds good," without too much of a sarcastic tone creeping into his voice. He continued on, keeping low with his head on a swivel.

He made it to the fence and slipped under the spot they'd found earlier.

Another round of gunfire thundered and he ducked behind an old junker, thinking they'd spotted him.

But no. It was just more of the same.

A nearly-full moon cast a dim light on the surroundings, enough for him to make his way through the maze of discarded junk. He edged to the corner of an outbuilding and peeked around.

In the relatively open space at the front of the

property, a scene like he never expected to witness in real life was, in fact, happening in the flesh.

In the flesh, literally. Some of the men were running around in underwear. A few of the women were missing their tops. Several barrels had been gathered and placed in the middle. Bright orange fires burned in each of them. A half-circle of flaming black rubber stuck out of the top of one. The burning tires left a biting, choking stench thick in the air.

As disturbing as all that was, it didn't hold a candle to the main attraction and, he realized, the reason for the gunfire.

Hanging from a tall pole erected next to the front gate was Eugene. Rather, Eugene's bullet-riddled corpse. They'd lashed his dead body to the end of the pole and raised it for their sick amusement.

One of the half-dressed men staggered over and stuttered to a stop below the corpse. He pointed a handgun up and fired off a few rounds. None obviously hit their target and the rest of the partiers howled with laughter. The shooter tried again and this time hit the dangling carcass that had once been a tinkerer named Eugene.

Cade didn't have any love for the man, but that didn't mean he approved of this. It turned his stomach, made him sick to the core. Violent thoughts passed through his mind, but he let them pass in silence. He wasn't there to right all the wrongs. He wasn't there to mete out justice to those who so plainly deserved it.

No, he was there to get their stuff.

Nothing more.

Nothing less.

Unfortunately, even that far simpler task looked all but impossible at the moment. There were in fact at least fifty people gathered round. Every single one of them was armed. Handguns, rifles, shotguns, knives. There was a small armory's worth of firepower in evidence.

While he, on the other hand, carried a single pistol.

Any kind of direct assault was doomed to fail. Maybe they could sneak in after the party died down and everyone eventually passed out. But even then, all it would take was for a single voice to raise the alarm and unleash a hornet's nest that stung with bullets.

There had to be a better way.

And then he thought of it.

Nothing was going to be a guarantee, but this would at least give them a chance.

He needed to tell the others so they would be ready. He turned to head back.

Unfortunately, he turned right into a handgun pointed at his head. The Puckett who shot down Eugene in cold blood. And he looked ready to do the same to Cade.

"Where in the hell do you think you're going?"

50

A mouth full of bad teeth grinned at him. Some yellow, others black with decay. "Drop it."

The last thing in the world Cade wanted to do was drop his weapon.

"Okay," Rotten Mouth said as an evil light flared in his eyes. He wanted to shoot.

Cade let the pistol fall out of his hand.

The guy shrugged. "Guess you live, for now. If you want to keep it that way, best move real slow. Now, turn around and let's go show everybody what I found."

Cade glanced down and saw an iron bar leaning up against a stack of tires.

Rotten Mouth followed his eyes, which was exactly the idea.

Cade ducked and drove forward into him. He wrapped him up and delivered a double leg take down like he hadn't done since his college wrestling days.

He arched up and then drove him down into the dirt. His shoulder ramming through Rotten Mouth's solar plexus. That got the reaction he was hoping for.

The breath exploded out of Rotten Mouth's lungs. His chest convulsed for air, but he wasn't able to draw in another breath.

Straddling his stomach, Cade reared back and smashed a fist into his face. And then another to the side of the jaw.

The guy's head whipped to the side. Blood and teeth flew out.

Cade pulled back for another strike, but didn't get the chance to deliver it.

Something walloped him in the side of the head. He tumbled over into the dirt. Blinking and dazed and wondering why his whole head was filled with agonizing vibrations.

Rotten Mouth was groaning and laughing, blood pouring out of his mouth.

Cade rolled onto his back and waited for everything to come into focus.

A dark figure stood above him holding a sawed off shotgun in hand. A gruff laugh and his pocked face came into focus. "He done beat the piss out of you, Murph! Just look at you!" More raspy laughter.

Murph was slowly pushing up to a sit. He snarled and spoke in a slurred voice. "Help me find my gun! I'm going to kill this bastard."

Cade was still trying to stop the ringing in his head. Still waiting for his arms and legs to feel like they were connected to his body. The feeling seeped back into his limbs like thick oil. They were there, but they were heavy and slow and he couldn't trust that they'd do what he needed them to.

A spear of despair went straight through his heart.

If he died here in this remote speck of nowhere, his daughter would be on her own. His family would be on their own. He would disappear from their lives and they would never know what had happened. And worse, he wouldn't be there to protect them.

He spotted a handgun in the shadows under a rusted hubcap. If he could just reach it in time.

He stretched out an arm, but it was moving at quarter speed and the guy standing over him saw it from a mile away.

Fight the Shock

He hopped over and stepped a boot down on Cade's wrist. He put his full weight on it too.

Cade groaned. Stupid arm was working good enough to feel the pain but not enough to get the gun.

Another shadow emerged from behind the stack of tires.

Another drugged up partier come to help finish him?

The figure picked up the iron bar and swung as the guy with the shotgun was turning to see who'd come.

The bar landed flush to the side of his head. It hit with a sickening crunch that guaranteed the skull was shattered. He slumped to the ground.

The shadow stepped into a pool of dim orange fire light.

It was Hudson.

Another swing and Hudson turned Murph's lights out a second later. Hudson knelt down next to Cade. "Are you okay?" He grabbed him by the shoulder and helped him sit up.

Cade groaned through it but made it up. "I thought I told you to stay outside the fence?"

"I know, but you were taking forever and I figured you might need some help."

Cade nodded. "Looks like you were right." He reached up a hand and Hudson hauled him to his feet. It took a second to steady himself, but then he was good. More or less. "We need to set up a diversion to have any chance at getting our things back."

"Do you have something in mind?"

"I do."

"Are they dead?" Hudson asked, his voice trembling.

Cade didn't know for certain and didn't much care either. They were either gone or would be soon. The tone in the kid's voice though made him keep that to himself for now.

"Help me drag them over there," he said pointing to the inky black space between an outbuilding and a twisted heap of ruined fenders.

They took the weapons and deposited the bodies where they wouldn't be discovered. With that sorted, they crept away to rejoin Wesley in the woods.

51

Hours passed as they waited in the forest. The sounds of the raucous party within the fence slowly died down and eventually went quiet.

And then it was time to move.

They each had an objective and Cade had to complete his to make the other two possible. He now had the shotgun and Hudson had a handgun, both taken from the two partiers that Hudson had taken out.

Cade squirmed under the fence and kept a look out while the other two followed. Once inside, they didn't have to say a word. Their missions were clear. Now, it was time to execute.

With a curt nod, Cade crept away into the shadows. The flaming tires in the barrels had burned down and now only dim pools of orange kept the black of night at bay. His biggest worry was clattering into something and waking up the whole lot of them before he was in position. Or accidentally stepping on a passed out drunk and having it end the same way.

So he took it slow. Carefully moving, eyes straining into the darkness at the indistinct shapes. He finally made it into position, a spot behind one of the trailers and facing the cache of five gallon propane tanks across the way. If this worked out like he hoped, they were about to witness a real fireworks show.

Passed out partiers laid around the open space surrounding the burn barrels. Couches and chairs dragged out from somewhere were occupied by others. Something higher up creaked and it was Eugene's desecrated body twisting in the breeze.

Cade took aim with the shotgun and fired.

Two quick shots and slugs punched through tanks.

The sharp hiss of expelled gas. A spark caught and a ten foot long jet of flame shot out the side.

Voices cried out as people woke up in surprise.

It was a distraction, but it wasn't nearly enough.

Cade fired two more times.

The sharp clang of impacted metal and the hiss of escaping pressurized gas. The tanks caught the flame of the first one and the fireworks picked up in earnest.

A spinning pinwheel of flame raked across a couch, lighting its occupants on fire. They leaped up, screaming and running. Human torches until they crumpled to the ground.

A man fled across the middle to get away. A tank rolled over and the flame hit full on. Like a welder's torch on metal. The flame consumed him.

And the smell.

It had been bad enough from the burning tires before. Now, it was worse. Thick, choking, repulsive.

One of the tanks ruptured and exploded. The concussive blast hit like a thunderclap. Fragments of the flaming tank shot into the air.

A figure raced toward the farm truck. It was Wesley following through on his part of the plan.

In the chaos, one of the invaders saw him and drew a pistol to shoot him.

Cade got the shot off first and hit him center mass. He was no longer a threat.

Wesley climbed up into the truck and started the engine. The headlights kicked on and the big diesel engine rumbled. He threw it into reverse and hit the gas. Tires spun kicking out fountains of dirt and the truck lurched backward. It crashed through the gate.

An invader with a rifle stopped in the center of the action and took aim at the truck. He fired and glass shattered before Cade knocked him down.

Cade cursed but was relieved to see that Wesley was okay when the tires turned and the truck straightened out on the road.

Even with the ruptured tanks spewing like flamethrowers, some of the invaders were starting to recover.

Where was Hudson?

Had something happened to him?

If they didn't get out of there quick, it was going to turn into a pitched battle and they were still vastly outnumbered and outgunned.

Twin lights swept around an outbuilding deeper in the property. An engine roared and the old GMC truck came into view. It swung sideways and took down a guy with a rifle. It smashed through a stack of tires and kept coming.

It hit one of the burn barrels, sending it rolling away and throwing out bits of smoldering tire as it went. The truck skidded to a stop and Cade was already in motion.

Shots fired and bullets pinged off the body as Cade dove into the open passenger door.

"Go!" he yelled as he slammed the door shut behind him.

Hudson hit the gas and the truck jumped forward.

The rear glass shattered and more bullets thunked into the tailgate.

They sped away and caught up with Wesley a little ways down the road. Still following the plan, they kept going. They didn't stop until they'd taken several turns and gone far enough to ensure they wouldn't be tailed.

The big farm truck slowed and pulled to a stop.

They followed suit and the three hopped out. Wesley shone a flashlight into the back of his truck. The bikes were gone. The AR-15 and their bags too.

Cade's mood was quickly turning sour. The elation of escape falling into frustration. He kicked at a pile of tarp and his boot hit something underneath. He threw the tarp back and there it was.

His Get Home Bag.

He grabbed it up and slung it over his shoulder. By the weight of it, he knew it hadn't been found. He hopped down out of the back to rejoin Wesley and Hudson.

And without having to say it, they all knew it was time for saying goodbye.

They shook hands and gave awkward hugs that were nevertheless full of earnest appreciation. Each for the other and all that had passed in their short time together.

"You boys be safe, okay?"

Cade nodded. "You too."

Wesley patted him on the shoulder. "I know you're going to find your daughter. She's lucky to have a father like you."

Cade swallowed hard. He wished he felt as certain. But he knew he couldn't, not until she was safely in his arms and he could be there to stand between her and whatever the world decided to throw their way.

What had she been through already?

Had it been anything like what he and Hudson had faced?

All he had were questions. No answers.

They all got in their vehicles and parted company. Wesley back to his farm and a peaceful corner of the world for as long as that lasted.

Cade and Hudson on the road to Las Vegas.

And if nothing went wrong, they'd be there before the sun came up.

52

Lily started the Beige Barfinator and eased out of the parking spot. The early morning sun lanced through receding shadows of the fifth level of the Mandalay Bay's parking garage. They'd dumped Donny's car behind the strip mall across the street and sprinted over. Security had helped them into their room. It had taken less than five minutes to gather their belongings, fill up on water and leave.

Right before leaving, she'd left a note in the room and one with the hotel reception desk. She had no idea where her father was or if he was still alive. But if he was alive, she knew he'd do everything possible to get to Las Vegas to find her. The notes would let him know that they were headed home.

Sleeping in the room overnight would've been more comfortable than sleeping in the car, but Lily hadn't trusted it. Her backpack was at Zeke's house and it had the keycard to their hotel room.

So there was a chance he could've paid them a visit while they slept. Or worse, Jax and his crew might've found out and busted their door down.

No, it was safer to sleep in the car so that's what they'd done. Though how much sleeping they actually got was an open question. After their nightmare of being trapped in the other parking garage, the slightest noise had them freaking out. But they'd survived the night and the sun had finally peaked above the eastern horizon.

Lily pulled out of the garage and stopped at the road. "Ready to go home?"

Piper nodded. "Las Vegas? Hate it. Worst bachelorette party ever. I'm never coming back. Why did I let you convince me into coming?" She made a weak grin and there was as much exhaustion and sadness in it as there was humor.

Lily forced a laugh. "Yeah, remind me never to do that again." She pulled out and found the entrance ramp to Interstate 15 north. Abandoned cars littered the road, but it looked passable. If it was possible to say anything good about the EMP attack, perhaps it was that it had happened after rush hour traffic.

They drove along the shoulder, cutting in and around where that was blocked. The traffic grew sparse as they reached the northern edge of the city. They passed under a green highway sign that had a red, white and blue badge with 15 North on it.

Nine hours and five hundred fifty miles to Durango. They had a full tank but it would take more than one to get there.

Lily glanced over at Piper.

She had her window cracked and gusts of wind blew through her hair. The morning sunshine painted her face in warm pastel hues. Her mouth carried the smallest hint of a smile. A real one.

They'd actually done it.

They'd made it out of the city.

Survived unimaginable horrors to get this far.

And now they were on their way home.

She wanted to be back in Durango more than anything. Before the events of the last two and half days, she wouldn't have thought much of the drive home. It was just a matter of doing the miles and getting it over with.

Now however, she knew differently. Anything could happen.

And so they had to be ready.

53

An old logging road through Sequoia National Forest cut the travel miles in half. It should've cut the travel time too except Eugene's guaranteed-to-be-reliable-but-with-no-warranties-offered GMC truck went kaput on the outskirts of Las Vegas.

Getting over the pass north of Potosi Mountain had sucked the life out of it. They'd managed to coast at low speed a while longer, but it finally sputtered and died. Cade had looked it over and tried a few things, but it was done and he hadn't wanted to waste any more time on it.

And so they'd been following the 160 east for the last five hours. The sign for interstate 15 North showed it was just up ahead. Cade's rough calculation on the map showed that the Mandalay Bay

Hotel was another four miles to the north. He knew Lily's room number and so that was the destination. Another hour and a half to get to her.

If she was there.

If she was still alive.

Hopefully, the Volvo worked and they were already back home in Durango. She would've left a note if so. That was basic communication protocol. But maybe the car didn't work. Maybe something had happened. Maybe…

He couldn't let himself think much beyond getting there.

The sun was climbing higher in the sky with the afternoon heat settling over the city like a wool blanket.

Hudson trudged along beside, never slowing the pace. The kid had endurance. Physically and mentally. The physical kind wasn't a surprise considering he was an avid cyclist. He could ride fifty miles without blinking. But the emotional endurance had definitely been a surprise.

How long it would last or how deep that well went, Cade didn't know. But he admired the kid for holding up as well as he had considering the heavy burden he was carrying.

He dug a water bottle out of his bag and took a

few drinks. He passed it over to Hudson who did the same. "We should be there in less than two hours."

Hudson nodded as he surveyed the sprawling city. They walked a while longer before he broke the silence. "It's strange, but I never thought to ask. What's your daughter like?"

A lump formed in Cade's throat and he couldn't speak until it loosened up enough to swallow. "She's amazing. Strong. Smart. Resourceful. Kind. Loving. Stubborn as a mule, like her mother."

Hudson chuckled. "Sounds like someone else I know."

Cade made a face at him. "I just hope she's okay."

He didn't realize at first that he'd said it out loud.

"I do too," Hudson murmured.

Cade lengthened his stride. He'd beaten the odds and survived this far. Skill, determination and maybe a little luck, if he was being honest, had brought him to this city in the desert.

He was close.

Closer than seemed remotely possible when he and Hudson were bobbing in the waves out in the dark waters of the bay.

But he'd made it.

And he wasn't about to let anything stop him now.

Thanks for reading!

What happened to Wesley when he returned to his farm and that huge pack of lovable dogs?

Find out in the free epilogue by signing up to my newsletter below. You'll also receive one novel, one novella and one short story, all for free. You'll also be the first to know about new releases, bonus content and more.

TAP HERE TO GET THE EPILOGUE

THANKS

This book wouldn't be what it is without the help of numerous wonderful readers. Their input has been invaluable. I want to personally thank Danielle, Wayne, Genelle, Cheryl, Ilona, and Patti for giving feedback on the beta version of this book. You folks are awesome! And you deserve a poem.

Rosés are pink
Violas are brown
You all are amazing.
You're the toast of the town!

Thank you so much!

WANT FREE BOOKS?

Want one novel, one novella and one short story, all for free? You'll also be the first to know about new releases, bonus content and more.

Go to WWW.WILLIAMODAY.COM to find out more.

OTHER WORKS

World in Collapse
FIGHT THE SHOCK, Book 1

Extinction Crisis Series
SOLE CONNECTION, a Short Story

SOLE PREY, a Prequel Novella

SOLE SURVIVOR, Book 1

SOLE CHAOS, Book 2

THE TANK MAN, a Short Story

THE PLUNGE, a Short Story

ZOMBURBIA, a Short Story

Edge of Survival Series
THE LAST DAY, Book 1

THE FINAL COLLAPSE, Book 2

THE FRAGILE HOPE, Book 3

Into the Dark Series
THE DARK DESCENT, Book 1

THE DARK UNKNOWN, Book 2

The Best Adventures Series

THE SLITHERING GOLIATH, Book 1

THE BEEPOCALYPSE, Book 2

THE PHARAOH'S CURSE, Book 3

THE INVISIBLE CRIMINAL, Book 4

THE DAY OF YES!, A Short Story

Short Stories

I KNOW THAT YOU KNOW

#MURDER

DOUBLE AGENT

THE GENDER LOTTERY

SAINT JOHN

SHE'S GONE

QUESTIONS OR COMMENTS?

Have any questions or comments? I'd love to hear from you! Seriously. Voices coming from outside my head are such a relief.

Give me a shout at william@williamoday.com.

All the best,
Will